I0690186

Humiliation

First Edition

Published by The Nazca Plains Corporation
Las Vegas, Nevada
2008

ISBN: 978-1-934625-58-3

Published by

The Nazca Plains Corporation ®
4640 Paradise Rd, Suite 141
Las Vegas NV 89109-8000

PUBLISHER'S NOTE
Humiliation is a work of fiction created wholly by *Christopher Trevor's*
imagination. All characters are fictional and any resemblance to any persons
living or deceased is purely by accident. No portion of this book reflects
any real person or events.

Cover Photo, Tomasz Trojanowski
Art Director, Blake Stephens

Dedication

To Justin Tyler Ormond, thank you
for friendship, inspiration and images

Humiliation

First Edition

Christopher Trevor

Contents

Introduction

Greetings constant readers and welcome to all new readers. My name is Christopher Trevor. If you are familiar with my works you know that in a lot of my stories the factor of "Humiliation" truly plays into the scenes I create. With that in mind I thought that a book of stories where humiliation is the main subject should be in order. Read how a butch cop is humiliated when he is overpowered after trying to make a routine arrest. A handsome and exotic model modeling a bikini finds sexual humiliation to be a strange and arousing turn-on. A lifeguard on duty at the beach suddenly and humiliatingly has his Speedo bathing trunks confiscated, in a most unusual manner at that. Humiliation is a state of disgrace, or loss of self-respect. It is strong feelings of embarrassment, an instance in which the person is caused to lose his or her prestige and self-respect. Humiliation is to reduce to a lower position in one's own eyes or others' eyes. It is related to the word "humble", and it is possible for one to be humiliated and not humbled...

Further thoughts on Humiliation from tickle hero/victim: Timmy Backman:

Christopher Trevor captured (literally) my interest a couple of years ago. The subject then was mostly tickling. Since then, he and I have collaborated on a number of stories in that genre. We have expanded beyond just tickling at this point. Now, Christopher puts pen to paper...or should i say fingers to keyboard and launches into a subject that, while different from our tickling stories, it can be and is tied (pun possibly intended) to the sexual psyche of the dominant and submissive...as well as male and female. That subject is "Humiliation." Humiliation can be a true turn-on for both the dominant who is dishing out the humiliation as well as for the dominated or humiliated. Humiliation is extremely exciting to us, the reader, the voyeur, looking in on the scene and reading and salivating as the dominant, the trickster, the controller, dominates and humiliates his subject. I suppose it can be said that it is my plight as a natural subordinate to be sexually stimulated by these scenes and stories. I look forward with penal anticipation on reading Christopher Trevor's latest set of tales dealing with yet another sexual stimulant...HUMILIATION.

Officer Mike Smith

Name: Smith, Police Officer Mike Smith

Badge Number: 52893

Age: Twenty-four

Situation: Code Red! Code (Fucking) Red, Sir!

     My name is Smith, Mike Smith to be exact. I'm a New York City police officer and damned proud of it bud, let me tell you. Sitting here, chewing and smoking my big fat cigar, looking through my "cop photo album" I can't tell you enough how proud I am to be a New York City police officer. My father had been a police officer and my grandfather had been a police officer *and* my grandfather's father had been a police officer. I was more than proud to have followed in my family's tradition. Fuck man, at twenty-four years of age *I had it all.* Well, lets just say I was happy with all that I had. Robust, somewhat ruggedly handsome and mean looking all at the same time, I have dark buzzed very short cut hair. I'm just about as bald as a marine boot camp drill instructor and I can be just as mean as one too bud, sure as shit, sure as fucking shit. With my attitude and dedication to the job *I knew* I would make sergeant in less than a few years. Six feet tall and built like a brick shit house from the daily workouts that I torture myself through at the Iron gym keeps my hairy body just like that, totally fucking iron-like. After working my long foot-beat shift each day I high tail it over to the gym and spend a little more than three hours working out, pumping iron. Fuck bud, two hundred and ten pounds of solid muscle on my six-foot frame and the face of a somewhat ruggedly handsome actor. Sitting there looking through my photo album I came across a picture taken of me in what had to be the most humiliating experience of my life. Why I kept that picture and a few others somewhat like it I'll never know. The event that occurred that night a little more than two years ago at this point changed my life; changed it totally bud. It was the most mortifying, kinkiest, yet most life altering experience I could have ever had. Chewing the rancid cigar as it smoldered in my craw I thought of how I never smoked until that fateful night. Cops have it more than pretty stressful let me tell you man, based on some of the stories and shit that I could tell you that I've seen over the years. Granted, you read a lot of stuff in the newspapers that happens to people. But cops see shit that happens that never makes it into the newspapers or onto the evening news *let me tell you*. The shit that happens to some people shouldn't happen to anybody bud. But nothing, *nothing* like what I want to tell you about that happened *to me* on that fateful night could have prepared me for the experience I had at the hands of a street tough thug named Freddy, Freddy Lopez to be exact. Looking at the photograph of myself in the most degrading of situations I wondered again why the fuck I had even kept the damned thing. Fuck, looking at that picture brought it all back to me…

It was mid September, the weather in New York had turned fairly and unusually cool, but not so cool that some people still didn't frequent the public parks. I was on my foot-beat, routinely patrolling Washington Square Park, dressed in my tight fitting navy blue police uniform, (my muscular chest and my thickly veined arm muscles straining against my neatly pressed long sleeved shirt) complete with black patent leather lace-up cop shoes. None of those black Reebok sneaker-like shoes that my police buddies wear nowadays. For me it was the traditional look of black patent leather shoes, shined so fucking bright and high that you could see your goddamned reflection in them. The time was approximately eleven thirty PM. Because of the fairly cool weather the park was just about deserted, but as I would soon find out, not totally deserted. As I was walking I suddenly heard the sounds of soft moaning and grunting a few yards ahead of me. Walking stealthily now I crouched into some bushes and then saw where and whom the moaning was coming from. On a park bench under a lamppost I saw that two guys were going at it big fucking time. I nearly gagged at the sight before me. One of the guys was sitting on the bench while the other one was on his knees on the concrete, sucking the guy on the bench off.

"Fucking faggots," I whispered angrily through clenched teeth. "Can't believe these two pansies are being brazen enough to do their perverted deeds right out in public like that."

From what I was able to see the faggot having his cock sucked had a monster-sized member, even bigger than mine, which is eight inches long, when it's soft. The guy sucking the big cock of the guy on the bench looked like he was struggling just to get the damned tube steak in and out of his mouth, yet somehow enjoying it at the same time. I could not believe that the guy sucking cock was enjoying having his mouth being raped the way it was. I didn't move to arrest them on the charge of performing an indecent act in a public place. For whatever the reason I was rooted to the spot. From what I could discern from my crouch in the bushes the guy sitting on the bench having his monster-sized cock sucked was tall with silky black hair pulled back in a pony tail, sort of Spanish looking actually. The one on his knees was a little shorter with blond hair, a real pansy queen as far as I was concerned. I watched and watched until the big guy shot his load all over the blond guy's tee shirt, his face and the knees of his jeans, grunting and groaning, shaking in ecstasy as he did so. The guy had his big meat stick in one hand and was stroking his mess all over the blond guy's face as he held him tight by the back of his neck.

"Ohhhhrrr man, fuck yeah, that was more than fucking awesome!" the big lug said, sounding like a construction worker after a hard day of slinging two by fours and swinging sledge hammers.

He was caressing the guy's blond hair, running his fingers through his mess on the guy's face and feeding it to him, making the blond queen eat it. I had a look of out right revulsion on my face in the bushes as the blond guy chowed heartily on the big lug's spunk. Fuck man, I wouldn't eat my own jazz after shooting a load, let alone chow down on some street thug's creamy mess. Although I have to mention that I'd been with a few cock hungry women that were just too glad to chow down on my cop slop, let me tell you bud. Then, the blond guy leaned down to kiss the big guy's black construction boots a few times each. I really grimaced in disgust and nearly blanched at the sight of that let me tell you. I mean, *kissing a guy's boots? What was up with that shit?* While his boots were being paid the respect he obviously thought they deserved the big guy packed his softening giant cock back into his jeans.

"Get goin' now Dennis!" the mean looking burly guy said sternly, leaning back on the bench, his big muscular chest pressing against his tight fitting white tee shirt. "You had the fucking privilege of sucking me off. Fuck man, I even let you put your goddamned mangy lips and tongue on my boots. *Now beat it!"*

Still crouched in the bushes I could not believe the way the arrogant son of a bitch was treating the blond guy. The blond pansy then got to his feet and told the big guy that he would hopefully see him again soon, and walked off. The big muscle-bound lug sat there looking up at the sky, rubbing his crotch a few times and swooning. That was when I decided to make my move. I stood up and walked slowly and methodically over to the bench. I pushed my police uniform hat a few inches back on my head, not wanting the brim of the thing obscuring my vision when I confronted this faggot punk. When I was standing directly in front of and over the guy was when the muscled street tuff noticed me. Actually, I was sure he noticed me as I had approached. He just didn't seem bothered about the presence of an officer of the law.

"Ah shit," the guy whispered, sounding more irritated than scared at the sight of a cop.

Up close I could see that the guy was very street credible, a real low life of sorts if ever there was one, *and* a faggot at that too. I could not believe that this tough street dude was a goddamned queer. He had deep sinister looking eyes. It was going to be a pleasure to arrest this goddamned faggot rapist, or to at least put the fear of the lord in him.

"Don't you know that sex in public places is against the law Faggot?" I asked the guy, propping one of my big feet up on the bench, next to where he was sitting.

"Yeah? So where do you think you and I should go Cop?" the guy asked me in reply, looking down at my foot on the bench, seeming to be checking his reflection in my shiny patent leather shoe.

"I could arrest you for indecency *and* based on that comment you just made Pansy," I said sternly. "Propositioning a police officer is *also* against the law."

The guy licked his lips and looked up at me blankly. For a brief second, maybe two he seemed to drink in the sight of my face.

"You watched it all huh Cop?" the guy asked me in a husky street sounding voice. "You watched as this faggot pansy got his big dick sucked and slurped on and got his rocks off huh? You think I didn't know that you were hiding in those bushes? Fuck man, *I hear everything that happens in this park.* But when you didn't move to arrest us I knew you were enjoying the show. So, did you get to see it all cop?"

"Never mind that you goddamned pervert," I seethed.

"So, are you going to arrest me then?" the guy asked, seeming not at all concerned, looking down again at my spit shined shoe on the bench.

"I should, but it would be your word against mine," I seethed through clenched teeth. "There were no witnesses except myself. You could claim that I saw you there and decided to pick on you. Faggots are always saying that police officers pick on them. The way things are going lately for cops the case would go on and on. Probably I'll let you off with a warning."

I put my foot back down on the ground and as I was reaching behind myself for my citation pad on my utility belt the guy sitting on the bench said, "And I'll let *you* off with this." With a real mean looking smirk on his face and before I even knew what was happening, while I reached for my citation pad the guy made a hard and tight fist. He brought the fist down hard on my crotch, sucker punching my balls good and hard.

"Arrrrrrrrrrrrhhhhhh!" I screamed like a suddenly trapped lion and whirled around stupidly in blinding and excruciating pain.

As I whirled around, doing a stupid dance of pain my police hat flew off my head and to the ground. Before I knew what the fuck was happening I had been relieved of my baton, seemingly like magic. The guy used my baton to give me a second shot to my poor already wounded balls.

"AYYYYYYYRRRR!" I screamed again, my voice echoing through the deserted park, this time falling to my knees in front of the guy, my hands instinctively over my crotch.

Fuck, it felt as if my poor balls had just been turned into a massive quivering mess of jelly.

"Heh, they should make you cops wear protective baseball cups down there on your privates," the guy laughed meanly, reaching down and helping himself to my service revolver, sticking it in his belt. "You never know when some pansy faggot is goin' to make a move for your meat. Fuck, nothin' is better than seeing a big tough guy take a hit or two in the gonads, heh."

The guy, still smirking stepped behind me, loomed menacingly over me and rubbed the tip of my baton over my more than muscular back.

"Poor dumb cop," the guy murmured. "It sure as shit looks to me like you really need to be taught a hard lesson where respect for people's stations in life is concerned."

As I writhed in blinding pain, half listening to the street mug prattle on, the thug helped himself to my handcuffs, taking them off the clip on my utility belt. My breath heaving, not even yet having realized that I had been relieved of my gun I reached into my empty holster, my hand trembling.

"*Shit,*" I seethed softly, realizing my now totally dreadful situation.

The guy whacked my hand hard with my baton, getting a good loud grunt of pain out of me. Then, he yanked my hands roughly behind me.

"Wh-what the fuck are you doing man?" I gasped in shock at this twisted turn of events.

"Like I just said, you need to be taught a hard fucking lesson Cop," the guy repeated. "Oh, and as of now you are officially off duty for the night."

I thought for sure that he was planning on killing me. Shit, what a way for my short-lived career as a cop to end up I thought miserably. But, obviously he didn't kill me. No, this street tuff thug had other plans where I was concerned. He snapped my handcuffs onto my wrists, locking my hands behind me. Next, he confiscated my utility belt and hooked it around his own waist, putting my gun back in the holster. Looking up at the thug, finally having caught my breath, my balls still aching beyond miserably however, I yelled, "*This shit is against the law Faggot! Release me now!*"

"Not till you've learned a very much needed lesson you goddamned homophobic cop!" the guy seethed and cuffed me hard across the jaw, sending me sprawling to the ground.

"Uuuuuhhhhhhhhffff!" I grunted as I hit the ground, my legs splaying out good and wide, giving the thug an open invitation to my already wounded balls.

With a smirk on his face he gave me a good kick in the balls with the tip of his black construction boot.

"Hoooooofffffff!" I sputtered stupidly, instinctively locking my legs together, my feet off the ground, my eyes rolling in my head. *"F-fucker…"*

My balls felt like they were swollen to twice their size as the guy reached down, grabbed the center of my tie and twined it snugly in his fingers. He hauled me to my feet and straightened my tie for me. He was looking at me hungrily and lustfully, the spot on my jaw where he'd cuffed me starting to bubble up.

"Get your mangy and perverted hands off me Faggot!" I seethed breathlessly and in total pain and anger. "I've got you on three accounts of assault on a police officer, restraining a police officer and performing an indecent act in a public place."

Smiling, looking at my nametag the guy said, "By the time this long night is over you'll be begging me to put more than my hands all over you Officer Smith!" Still smiling, the guy placed a hand over my crotch, my wounded balls and was totally surprised to find the (fear) hard-on I was sporting in my uniform pants.

"And from the look and feel of things down here you have a meaty hard-on in your uniform trousers," the guy said mockingly.

I hunched my shoulders up, the muscles in them straining against my uniform shirt as the guy slowly rubbed my hard-on and aching balls. I glared at the guy as he gave my beefy manhood a squeeze through my pants. The pain in my balls sped through my very being as he rubbed them. I had all to do just to stay balanced on my feet, clenching my teeth in out right misery.

"Looks like you're just about as beefy and thick as I am Cop," the guy said, still rubbing my hard-on, then taking me by my upper arm, his big hand almost making it totally around my bulging and muscular biceps. "My car is this way. *Let's get goin' Cop!*"

"Wait!" I blurted loudly, starting to feel real and total fear at that point, my (fear) hard-on dripping pre cum in my shorts now. *"Just where the fuck do you think you're taking me?"*

"Officer Smith, I am going to take you on the ride of your more than sorry life," the guy replied with a fiendish looking grin on his face.

"You aren't taking me anywhere Faggot!" I roared angrily and heaved myself out of the guy's grasp.

Prepared to run, but hating myself for even thinking it I was quickly dealt yet another hard blow to my balls with my baton.

"Hoooofffffff!" I hoofed, sounding almost like a big dog, my mouth turned into an "O" of surprise.

I again hunched my shoulders up and looked miserably at my captor as he calmly took me again by my upper arm.

"As I said, my car is this way," the guy said, walking me now limping toward his car.

As we passed the spot where my hat had fallen he picked it up and placed it haphazardly on my head.

"Goddamn it man, kidnapping a police officer is against the law and a federal offense at that you scum bucket, faggot!" I seethed miserably in a high pitched tone of voice, the pain emanating from my balls moving through me at what felt like thousands of miles per hour. "Not to mention assault on a police officer being against the law as well."

"Okay dumb cop, we won't mention it," the guy chuckled meanly.

We walked through the dark and deserted park to a car that was parked behind a cluster of some big trees. Holding my arm in a firm grasp the guy said, "Here we are." Admittedly I was shaking in my shoes as I watched the thug open the trunk of the car. He shucked my utility belt into the trunk and leaned down to click off my radio, my only port of communication to headquarters. Smiling meanly, he took the key to the handcuffs from my utility belt and deposited it in one of the pockets of his jeans He took my hat off me and chucked that into the trunk as well. Mostly I looked longingly at my gun, totally out of my reach with my hands cuffed behind me.

"Get in Officer," the guy said, grinning fiendishly.

"Oh no, *no,*" I whimpered miserably, breaking away from the guy again, again prepared to run and again hating myself for doing so.

But the guy was quick; I had very quickly come to realize that. He wasn't giving me up all that easily. He abruptly grabbed my necktie, pulled me close to himself and with his lips dangerously grazing mine he meanly said, "Get the fuck in." Moments later *I was in the trunk of the car,* curled up to make myself fit as comfortably as possible as the guy drove through the late night streets of New York City. *I had been kidnapped* I said to myself in the trunk of that thug's car. My worst and only fear since becoming a New York City police officer had come true, some big fucking goon had gotten the drop on me and literally kidnapped my sorry ass. And kidnapped by a goddamned faggot no less…

About ten minutes later or so (by my best estimates) the car had stopped in an alley behind a run-down and abandoned apartment building somewhere in the west village. I railed and ranted the word faggot over and over at the guy as he hauled me roughly out of the trunk and leaned me up against the side of his car. In what seemed like seconds my uniform pants were down around my ankles along with my white BVD briefs. With my balls still aching and looking like they were swollen to twice their goddamned size in my sweaty sac I watched in horror and forced ecstasy as the guy slid to his knees in front of me. He began sucking the fuck out of my big (fear?) hard beefy cop cock, running his hands up and down my muscular legs at the same time, snapping the elastic in my socks against my skin.

"Ohhhhhhhhh fuck, *fuck, you fucking pansy ass faggot*," I groaned. "Fucker, don't be sucking my damned meat stick! *I'm no faggot you bastard!*"

The thug took my cock out of his mouth for a moment and holding it in his hand looked up at me with a mean looking grin on his face.

"Heh, you might not be a faggot, but this harder than hard hard-on is saying otherwise dumb Cop! And I'm willin' to bet that no lady ever sucked you so fucking good!" the guy said angrily. "Oh, and for the record, when the time comes to arrest me my name ain't Faggot, it's Freddy. Freddy Lopez. If you still plan on arresting me when this is all over that is."

That said, Freddy gobbled my pre cum dripping cock back into his greedy and hungry mouth and resumed sucking it, nipping at the tip of it, making me cry out in a man's pain, and then sucking it some more. My wounded balls throbbed crazily as the guy worked my cock like it was a musical instrument he was playing. Looking down, watching as Freddy sucked and sucked my cop cock I could not believe, fuck, *I really could not believe that this had happened to me*, that some street thug had gotten the drop on me, trapped me and now had me in a state of somewhat ecstasy.

"Ohhhhhhhrrrrr man, fuck man, I-I'm goin' to cum Freddy," I suddenly gasped breathlessly.

Freddy took my big beefy and throbbing meat stick deeper into his craw, moved his hands up over my round somewhat hairy butt cheeks, gripped them hard and swallowed my mess heartily as I seemed to spew endless globs of cop sperm.

"Ohhhhhhhrrrrr g-god, fucking thug, fucking low life, eating my damned mess, making me shoot my goddamned load," I grunted as Freddy suckled the fuck out of my sausage-like cock.

Holding my butt cheeks in a firm grip each he pulled me deeper into his mouth, pushed me up to my tiptoes and sucked me harder still, gyrating me on my toes.

"Uhhhhhhhhrrrrr fuck," I seethed as the guy's tongue swirled over and over my hard shaft in his mouth as he didn't lose a drop of my mess.

When I was done he let go of my butt cheeks, lowered me from my tiptoes and let my cop cock slip slowly from his mouth as it softened, smacking his lips around it, sucking off the last droplets of my sperm.

"Nice big load Cop," Freddy commented snidely, licking his lips, looking up at me. "Real nice. Looks like you're in love with me already huh?"

I simply looked away from him as he pulled my briefs back up for me, patting my crotch as still some droplets of cum oozed from my slit and stained against my BVDs. I felt a sense of revulsion as the guy put my briefs back on me, more revulsion when he did that than when he'd captured me, assaulted my balls or sucked my cock. I then watched in a state of horror as the thug named Freddy pulled my uniform pants off me over my black patent leather shoes and navy blue knee length socks, ripping and tearing the pants a little in the process as he did.

"H-hey, what are you doin' Fag-er-Freddy?" I asked in terror as I was depantsed. *"I need my goddamned pants man!"*

"Not for where you're going you won't need them," the guy replied, again opening the trunk of the car.

He tossed my uniform pants into the trunk along with my utility belt and hat.

"Get in," he said to me commandingly.

He wasn't holding my arm in a firm grasp this time, but admittedly I didn't entertain any thoughts of running off at that point. Where would a cop go minus his pants and handcuffed after all? And I knew at that point that he would deal me another good shot to my poor balls if I tried running off. Shaking and trembling I climbed back into the trunk of the car and again curled myself up to fit. Freddy slammed the trunk closed, plunging me into sheer darkness. In moments we were again driving through the late night streets of New York. I shook in out right terror in the trunk, figuring that this thug meant to kill me when this was all over…

A while later the car stopped and again Freddy hauled me out of the trunk. I saw that we were in another alley behind another abandoned and run-down apartment building. And then, a few moments later Freddy was leaning against his car while I stood there against a brick wall, angry and handcuffed, having my big cop cock sucked alternately by two faggots.

"Ohhhhhhhrrrrrr shit Freddy, wh-what's the point of all this?" I grunted, my muscular shoulders hunched back, my massive chest and pecs pressing against my uniform shirt. "Making your faggot buddies here have at my goddamned meat stick?"

I noticed that one of the guys sucking me like crazy was the guy who had sucked Freddy off on the bench back in the park earlier. What a twisted turn of events I thought in a huff. At the time I had watched the guy sucking Freddy's cock I never once entertained a thought of him having at my big meat stick.

"That's it you wussies, suck that cop's dick," Freddy said to the two guys as I stood there helplessly with my over-sized cop cock sticking out of my cum stained BVD under shorts. "I promised you two a big surprise, *well, here it is.* And yeah Cop, it looks like I'm turning you into some cheap ass whore huh?"

"I see lots of years in jail ahead of you Freddy," I grunted in fury and a mix of forced ecstasy. "Fuck man, I got you on assault, kidnapping and not to mention rape!"

The two guys squeezed my wounded balls through my under shorts as they took turns sucking and suckling my big cop cock, getting a few good loud grunts of torment out of me.

"Yeah, you got me Cop," Freddy chuckled. "You're the police officer with his wrists locked in his own handcuffs, you're the schmuck cop without his uniform pants, you're the one with the wounded balls having his big boner sucked like some cheap hustler, yeah, *you really got me.*"

After Freddy said that I simply watched and grunted as the two wussies (as Freddy had called them) greedily sucked my cop cock like crazy. They chowed down on it like their lives depended on it, deep throating it, sliding their mangy tongues all over the shaft of it, soaking it real liberally with their saliva. They drooled all over it and sucked their saliva off my big meat stick, sending chills and thrills through my very being as they locked lips around my slimy shaft.

"Ohhhhhhhrrrrrrr shhhhiiiiiittt," I grunted throatily, looking angrily over at Freddy as he puffed a rancid and stinking cigar. "I swear man, I swear to God, when I get out of this you are going to pay big fucking time for all of it Freddy!" What is this shit, making your faggot friends suck my big cock? You think I'm some piece of beef you can just hock at the nearest exchange?"

Freddy simply smiled meanly, puffed and smoked his cigar and watched as his buddies sucked and sucked and sucked my cock.

"Fuck it all man, my big cop cock isn't for you *or for any of your faggot friends* to be making sport with," I railed.

Freddy watched intently as his buddies worked my big cock.

"Man Officer Stupid Smith, you still don't have a shred of a clue where all this is leading do you?" Freddy asked me, a smirk on his face, his cigar jammed in the side of his mouth.

"Ohhhhhhh fuck, fuck, getting close now you cock hungry bastards! G-God almighty Freddy, my damned balls are aching in my under shorts you fucker!" I panted in total disbelief not having acknowledged what Freddy had just said (spat?) to me. "C-can't fucking believe this shit, that two mangy faggots are making me shoot my damned load of cop spunk."

One of the guys quickly slurped my throbbing cock deep into his mouth and sucked me greedily as his faggot buddy toyed with my nipples through my uniform shirt, twisting and squeezing them. I shot my second load of cop goop for the night, down a second faggot's throat no less.

"Ohhhhhhhhhhhh shhhhiiiiiittt, yeah, ohhhhhrrrr god," I howled in the forced ecstasy as my mess of sperm felt as if it were being siphoned from me.

"Perverts, fuckers..."

"Nice sexy load Cop," the guy who had swallowed my mess said, grinning up at me when I was done, my slimy semi hard cock dangling in his face.

Freddy told his two buddies to beat it, just as he had treated the guy earlier who had sucked his cock, the same guy who had just sucked my cop mess down his throat. He stood there watching as his two buddies walked off, holding my upper muscular arm in a firm hammer lock-like grasp.

"L-let me go man," I grumbled miserably as Freddy straightened my tie for me and then packed my slimy cop cock back into my under shorts, not handling me all that gently down there, his smoldering and stinky cigar sticking out of the side of his mouth. "You're already in a shit load of trouble Freddy. Let me go now and it won't get any worse."

"I ain't in half a shit load of trouble as you are Officer Stupid Smith," Freddy said mockingly, held his cigar to my trembling lips and made me puff it a few times before ordering me back into the trunk of his car.

As we again rode around the late night streets of New York City I cringed in total fear in the trunk of Freddy's car. Fuck, what was to become of me at this point? The guy had kidnapped me and had sucked my cock *and* two of his faggot buddies had sucked my cock. As I thought of that my somewhat spent cop cock hardened in my under shorts. What was up with that shit anyway? I had noticed more than a few times some of my cop buddies checking out my bigger than big manhood in the locker room while we'd be getting changed from civilian attire to our police uniforms. I always attributed that to jealousy more than anything else though. I mean, my cop buddies couldn't have been thinking about sucking my cock and swallowing my juices could they? I mean, none of my cop buddies were faggots, *were they?* I mean, guys always checked out each other's cocks in the locker room, *didn't they?*

The next time Freddy let me out of the trunk I saw that we were parked across the street from a very sleazy leather type bar in a run-down part of the west village.

"Man oh man are my leather buddies in there going to love you Cop," Freddy said to me, trailing a fingertip over the puffiness on my face where he'd cuffed me earlier.

Leather buddies? Leather buddies? Fuck, the way I'd heard it told through the years these leather pervs had a real hot spot for police officers. And this fucking faggot was planning on bringing me into a goddamned leather bar? He again straightened my tie, smoothed out my uniform shirt, getting rid of the wrinkles I had made in it laying in the trunk of the car and squeezed my fat nipples under my shirt also. Then, to my utter and total humiliation Freddy squatted down and pulled my socks up for me. My cock pounded in (fear?) my under-shorts.

"Freddy, never mind my damned socks, listen to me man, *don't bring me in that place like this!*" I pleaded helplessly. "Fuck, don't bring me in there at all man!"

Freddy simply smiled that mocking smile again, puffed the last of his cigar in my face and ground it out against my shiny badge.

"Fucker, that's how much respect you got for an officer of the law's badge eh faggot?" I asked him angrily.

Freddy held the butt of his smelly unlit cigar to my lips and before I realized what he planned to do he shoved the rancid thing into my mouth.

"Ulppp!" I gagged as the taste of the cigar butt filled my craw.

"Chew that up and swallow it Cop," Freddy said to me meanly. "I don't want to be given a ticket for littering if I drop it on the ground."

"Naw fucking way," I prattled miserably and was about to spit the stogie out when suddenly Freddy gave me a good punch to the gut. "Hoooooofffffff!"

My breath was literally knocked out of me and I involuntarily bit down on the cigar butt in my mouth. My mouth filled with rancid cigar paper and ashes. I stood there slightly doubled over in pain, chewing on the cigar as Freddy squeezed my wounded balls through my under shorts, holding them tight.

"Eat it cop, eat my goddamned cigar," Freddy said, watching triumphantly as with a look of agony on my face I did as he said.

When the cigar was gone my mouth tasted rancid and awful. I licked my lips and managed to stand up straight. Freddy let go of my balls and they throbbed miserably and in pain in my under shorts.

"Let's go Cop," Freddy said then. "It's time to introduce you to my leather and fetish buddies."

"C'mon man, give me my goddamned pants Freddy!" I pleaded desperately, knowing I was going into the leather bar despite my pleas.

Ignoring me, Freddy took me firmly by the arm and walked me quickly across the street.

"*Shit,*" I whispered angrily through clenched teeth, the taste of ashes filling my mouth and throat, my meat stick semi hard and all slimy in my white under shorts.

We walked into the bar. The place was somewhat crowded and very smoky. It smelled of cigar and cigarette smoke laced with the scent of marijuana as well. The underlying scent of liquor and beer was there as well. I saw men dressed in black leather from head to toe, men dressed in military uniforms from all branches of the service and some men simply dressed in black denim. Some of the men were restrained, handcuffed as I was, they were the leather slaves, the others, who were not restrained, were known as the leather masters, obviously like Freddy was to me at that moment. For anyone seeing us that sure was how it appeared. Some of the men were wearing leather hoods with eyes, nose and mouth openings, the hoods laced up behind their heads. I noted that there were various styles of the hoods as well. The slaves were clad in hoods that covered their entire head while the masters were wearing hoods that only concealed half of their face. I noticed that the majority of the men were wearing various styles of boots. My cop cock grew more than semi hard in my under shorts, betraying me. The bar was dimly lit, adding to the sinister atmosphere it boasted. Holding my arm tight Freddy walked me roughly up to the bar. I felt eyes all over me, checking me out, drinking me in, devouring me. I mean, how often was a cop brought into this place sans his uniform pants and captured *and* handcuffed by some street thug? But from what the men in the fetish and leather bar knew I wasn't a real cop. To them I was just some muscle bloke dressed up as a captured cop, acting out an erotic fantasy. Somehow I would have to make these faggots know the truth, if I were to escape Freddy that is.

"Hey Freddy my man, why ain't you dressed in your leather regalia tonight?" the black and extremely muscular bartender asked Freddy.

"I didn't have time to go home and change," Freddy explained to the bartender, who obviously knew him very well. "I got sidetracked after my usual stint down in the park."

As he spoke Freddy clutched my arm tighter, looking at me lustfully.

"So what'll it be for you and your… *underdressed* cop here?" the bartender with the iron like bare chest asked Freddy with a grin, seeming to be checking me out the way a lion checks out prey in the jungle.

The bartender looked to be a little better than six feet tall. The handsome shiny black skinned guy was wearing black leather pants, from what I could see on my side of the bar. I quickly took in the fact that he had muscles to spare, muscles rippled all over his torso actually. His chest and pecs were massively muscled and his nipples were as big and erect as two pencil erasers. Not a doubt in my mind that he was one of those queers who used vacuum pumps and snake bite clips on his nipples to get them that fleshy and erect. I also realized that if I happened to pass this big muscle dude on the street I would never have pegged him for a queer. What's the world coming to I wondered silently and my beef stick tingled in my under shorts.

"Give me a Bud and an empty glass for my cop," Freddy replied with a snicker. "When I have to piss I'll give him something to drink."

The bartender looked at me and laughed hysterically.

"I'm puttin' you on a piss diet Cop," Freddy said to me, squeezing my arm tighter.

"I am a New York City police officer!" I yelled angrily at the muscle bound bartender. *"This man has abducted me!"*

"Sure you are," the bartender replied, giving my bruised cheek a hard pinch. "So are the rest of the guys in here dressed up as cops."

The bartender placed Freddy's beer and an empty glass on the bar. Freddy took a hearty gulp of his beer and then looked at me, his captive cop.

"Don't make another stupid outburst like that again Cop," Freddy said to me sternly. "Or I'll make you sorrier than you already are."

Obviously telling people in the bar that I was a real cop was not going to work in getting me away from Freddy. Looking around the bar I saw some of the handcuffed guys being fed glasses of what looked like piss. Some of the handcuffed guys (the slaves) looked just too happy and ecstatic to be guzzling their master's rancid yellow liquid. I grimaced miserably, wondering if Freddy had been serious about making me drink his piss. My mouth already tasted bad enough from having been made to chew on and swallow Freddy's rancid stogie, but drinking piss would make my mouth taste and smell like a sewer for sure. I glanced at my captor as he sipped his beer and then looked at the empty glass on the bar, the glass that Freddy intended to use to feed me his piss with. My beef stick tingled long and (fear) hard in my under shorts…

At that moment two men dressed in the black leather regalia of masters walked over to Freddy and I. I stole a glance downwards and saw that they were both wearing engineer boots. They politely said hello to Freddy and he shook hands with both of them. From the way the two leathermen were looking so lustfully at Freddy I was slowly coming to realize that I'd been captured by someone who was held in very high esteem.

"This is one good lookin' police officer you have here Freddy," the first leatherman said, looking me over lustfully now, his teeth bared and grinning around a thick black goatee and mustache.

"His name is Smith," Freddy replied. "We just met tonight. He's my prize for the night, and maybe for tomorrow as well."

Standing there in my uniform shirt and tie, my under shorts, my knee length blue socks and black patent leather shoes and feeling ridiculous I looked at Freddy in total dismay over what he'd just said.

"Smith, lick my friend's boots," Freddy said to me with total authority.

With no choice other than to do as I was told I reluctantly got to my knees, leaned my upper body forward and stuck out my tongue. I licked each of the leathermen's boots a few times each, really putting my tongue to work on them. Jeez, back in the park I was repulsed watching the blond faggot lick Freddy's boots. Now it was I licking guys' boots and my hard-on hadn't subsided in the least. Fuck, what was up with all this shit??? As I licked the leathermen's boots Freddy sat down on a barstool. I saw my captor get comfortable, moved over to him on my knees, kissed his booted feet a few times each and then stood up. Freddy was looking me over with satisfaction mixed with lust showing in his eyes.

"Smith, there's a back room here," Freddy said to me. "I want you to go to that room with my two buddies here. When they're done with you *you're to come back to me.*"

I looked at Freddy in total alarm.

"Don't worry Cop, I'll have a nice frothy drink waiting for you when you get back," Freddy said mockingly, holding up the empty glass.

"It's not a glass of your goddamned piss that I was concerned about," I said despairingly as the two leathermen hooked their claw-like hands around my muscular arms. "Fuck man, don't be giving me out to your buddies like some cheap whore Freddy. This makes your situation that much worse man!"

The leathermen took me by my upper arms and walked me through the bar toward the back room that Freddy had mentioned.

"Listen to me you two *and listen fucking good,*" I said angrily through clenched teeth. "I really am a New York City police officer. This is no bullshit! Your friend Freddy back there abducted me in Washington Square Park when I intended to arrest him for performing an indecent act in a public place."

We moved closer toward the back room the two leathermen holding tighter and tighter to my muscular biceps as we walked. I noticed more and more men in the place really checking me out, taking in the sight of me. I figured that they were hoping that Freddy would give them a chance with me as well.

"Yeah, that's just what the guy that Freddy brought here last week said too, Cop," the leatherman on my right side said mockingly as we entered the back room. In the room it smelled dank and damp. The room was lit only by two dangling naked light bulbs.

"Okay Cop, get busy," the first leatherman said as they both took their big meat sticks out of their leather pants.

"I-I've never sucked cock before," I stammered angrily, looking in awe at the two big tube steaks I would soon be feasting on.

"I said get busy!" the leatherman said again, taking what looked like a flashlight from the back pocket of his pants. "There's no time like the present to learn!"

He flipped a switch on the tube-shaped device and pressed it against my poor wounded balls. Searing and blinding pain shot through my entire being and I suddenly found myself on my knees in front of the two leathermen. *Shit, shit, that was a goddamned cattle prod that that guy had just used on my damned balls.*

As I caught my breath and the pain in my balls intensified I found myself staring at two big pulsing thick and beefy tube steaks, two cocks that seemed to be looking at me like one eyed monsters. They were both more than relatively big, neither of them as big as Freddy's however. At the thought of Freddy's cock my dick grew harder in my under shorts, despite the awful pain my balls were in. I reluctantly stuck out my tongue and began by licking the tips of the leathermen's cocks as they dangled closely together in front of me. They tasted salty and smelled real funky of sweat, musty leather sweat. I also detected the taste of sour piss emanating from the slits of the two cocks. Then, I began sucking them alternately, the way the two faggots had alternately sucked me earlier. The two men towering over me moaned and grunted contentedly, kissing each other on the lips at the same time, slobbering in each other's mouth. The sounds of slurping filled the room as I worked each of the leathermen's cocks alternately. They were slow in cumming and I figured that they wanted to simply enjoy having their cocks sucked, to enjoy it as much and as long as possible. I sucked cock for the first time in my life that night and granted, I was a fast learner. Only because I didn't want that damned cattle prod to be used on my family jewels again. Mortified and feeling totally degraded I wondered what my father, his father and my great grandfather would have thought of me at that moment. I was totally sure that none of them had ever wound up in the clutches of a faggot leatherman and made into some kind of cheap hustler in a leather bar. I hunched my muscular shoulders up and strained the muscles in my biceps, my hands clenched into fists of anger as I sucked and suckled cock. I had a mouthful of the first leatherman's manhood when he shot his load first, right down my throat.

"RRRRmmmfffff!" I sputtered in alarm as my mouth and throat filled with the leatherman's mess.

"Ohhhhhrrrr yeah, fucking hot cop, eat my mess," the leatherman grunted, holding me tightly by the back of my big neck as he fed me his cum.

At first I was totally appalled as I was forced to guzzle and swallow the guy's spunk. But then, I realized that it didn't taste all that bad after all. As the guy shot what seemed like rope after rope of thick creamy sperm into my mouth I sucked and sucked on his big cock, scoffing it all down, swallowing almost greedily. My mind was by then a jumble of confusing questions. The second leatherman also made me swallow his spunk when he shot his load, not too long after his buddy had and not too long after savoring me sucking his meat stick for him.

"Oh man, that was fucking great!" the first leatherman said, packing his big cock back into his leather pants. "Not too bad for a guy who claims it's his first time out sucking cock."

"Do you think Freddy would mind if we got his cop off?" the second leatherman asked his buddy.

"Nah, lets milk the handsome guy," the first leatherman said.

Moments later, I found myself sitting atop a table with my feet up on the table and my legs spread wide. They had taken my big sausage-sized cock out of the fly opening of my BVD under shorts and were taking turns sucking it, running their mangy hands up and down my long muscular legs at the same time. Like Freddy had done earlier they snapped the elastic in my long socks against my skin.

"Ohhhhh yeah, fuck, *fuck it all you guys,* suck my big cop cock you two!" I heard myself saying, panting practically as the two leather guys took turns with my big meat in their mouths.

They squeezed my wounded balls in my under shorts and went on snapping the elastic in my tall socks and in my under shorts as well as they played suck with my big cock, bringing me closer and closer to orgasm.

"Ohhhhhhhrrrr gods," I crooned throatily. "What a night this turned out to be. Captured by a goddamned lunatic faggot and now being sucked off in a sleazy leather bar, of all things!"

It was a few minutes later when the two leathermen were still taking turns sucking my cock that I shot my third load for that night.

"Ohhhhhhhrrrr fuccckkkk man, yeahhhhrrr, got me creaming like a son of a bitch!" I blurted loudly as the first leatherman caught my jizz in his hand and then held it under my trembling lips.

"Eat up Cop," he said, holding his hand to my lips.

With no choice whatsoever in the matter I stuck out my tongue and licked my own cum off the first leatherman's hand and fingers, sucking at his fingers as I did so. The second leatherman packed my semi hard meaty cock back

35

into my under shorts, my poor balls still aching like crazy.

"Look guys, *you two have got to help me,*" I said desperately. "Freddy fucking kidnapped me, I'm telling you two the goddamned truth when I say that I'm a *real police officer!*"

Ignoring me the two men yanked me off the table top and literally pushed me out of the back room and back into the now very crowded bar. The door to the back room (where I'd just sucked cock and swallowed cum for the first time in my life) slammed shut behind me.

"Bastards!" I yelled at the closed door, standing there in my damned underwear and only part of my police uniform.

I angrily kicked the door and turned around facing the crowded bar. As I began to make my way slowly through the bustling bar I again felt eyes all over me, drinking in the sight of me, devouring me. A robust, burly looking guy dressed up in the formal uniform of a marine walked up to me and smiled mockingly, blocking my path.

"Hey Cop, looks like you lost your pants," he said to me, his eyes seeming to pierce me.

"Yeah, yeah, so I did," I mumbled angrily and walked past the marine.

Suddenly, the marine reached out and brazenly grabbed a few fingers full of one of my butt cheeks and squeezed and twisted it real hard, sending searing pain through me.

"*Hey!*" I snarled and turned back to the guy, facing him head on, my teeth clenched in total anger now.

"What are you going to do Cop?" the marine asked me snidely, running his fingers over my tie and my cigar ash smudged badge. "You're not really in much of a position to be cocky."

Then, he grabbing me by my tight melon shaped buns the marine pulled me to himself and kissed me hard on the mouth, forcing his thick tongue into my craw. The marine's tongue explored and probed my mouth and gums. The taste of Freddy's cigar and the leathermen's cum in my craw didn't seem to faze the guy in the least as he practically ate my face off me.

"RRRRRmmmffffff!" I moaned in anger as the marine kissed and kissed me, suckling my tongue till I thought for sure that he would tear it clear out of my mouth.

When the marine let go of me and sauntered off he had a look of out right satisfaction on his face. Panting angrily I looked toward the bar for Freddy and saw that he wasn't there. Shit, had he escaped? Even though I was in the position I was in it would still be my duty to arrest the guy before the night was over. But fuck, a guy had just kissed me on the lips I thought in a total rage. What a fucked up night this had turned out to be. Besides all of the other degrading things I had endured thus far I had just been smooched on the lips by some faggot dressed as a marine. Seeing as Freddy wasn't at the bar my eyes next found the exit. Okay, later for Freddy, first I had to get myself out of this damned sleazy bar, sans my uniform pants or not. I began to make a beeline for the exit, doing my best to get through the crowd, being groped as I passed by guys looking at me lustfully. When one guy (who was unaware of how badly my family jewels were hurting) grabbed my nuts through my under shorts I thought for sure I would go through the ceiling. I was almost to the door now, trying to ignore the awful pain in my poor balls. But then, as I was walking past the men's bathroom the door opened and my upper arm was roughly grabbed. I looked to my side and saw Freddy.

"Freddy!" I blurted, my dick tingling in fear in my under shorts.

"In here Cop!" Freddy said with total authority and yanked me roughly into the men's room, closing and locking the door.

So much for escaping I thought miserably when I saw that Freddy was holding a glass in his hand. It was half filled, with piss, yellow thick frothy looking piss.

"Freddy, listen to me man, *I mean it man, listen to me,* let's stop this now, *let's stop this now,*" I began, standing there feeling mortifyingly ridiculous in half my police uniform, my cop cock tingling in my sweaty under shorts. "You've kidnapped me man, *that is a federal offense! You put me in the trunk of your damned car! That's endangerment to my life! You've forced me to have sex without my consent, fuck man that's rape! Let me go now Freddy and maybe, just maybe, it won't be all that bad for you. Don't let me go and your situation gets that much worse man!*"

In response to my tirade Freddy put one big hand up behind my bull neck and held the glass of warm sour smelling piss to my lips with his other hand.

"Drink up Cop!" Freddy said with total authority, squeezing the back of my neck real tight, forcing my head downward toward the tall glass.

With my lips trembling and again, with no choice other than to do as I was being told, I drank Freddy's piss. It tasted like it smelled, rancid and sour and it was still very warm. No doubt Freddy had piss filled the glass just seconds before he snagged me into the men's room when I was making an attempt at escape.

"UCCCHHHH!" I gasped when I was done, Freddy having forced me to guzzle every drop of the yellow liquid in the glass.

He then looked at me hungrily, caressed my face with his hand, and said, "Damn it all, *much as you cops annoy the fuck out of me I got to say you are one fine looking dude Smith!*"

That said he clamped his lips down on mine and kissed my pissy tasting mouth. He forced his tongue deep into my mouth, sucked my tongue viciously and I felt his big hands roaming over my butt cheeks through my under shorts. When he stopped kissing me I looked at him as though it hadn't happened, as though I didn't have another hard on in my under shorts. Fuck me, I had cum three times that night and I was hard as a diamond and pulsing all over again in my damned under shorts! What was happening here???

"Freddy, please man, *do yourself a favor and release me now!*" I seethed at him, my mouth tasting of a horrid mixture of stale cigar, piss and the beer that Freddy had consumed earlier.

A deranged look then came over Freddy's face and he smiled more than fiendishly.

"Actually Cop, I have an idea," Freddy said. "And releasing you sure as shit isn't part of it."

Ten minutes later Freddy was exiting the men's room, *without me.* He had sat me on a toilet with the seat down in a stall that had no door on it. My under shorts were down around my ankles, my ankles tied and pulled apart with some rope that Freddy had found under the sink. Obviously I wasn't the first poor sap of a dude to be tied up in the stall. The rope pulled tight on my ankles forced me to keep my legs spread good and fucking wide, putting my big cop cock and wounded balls on display for all to see. The ends of the rope were tied off to pipes on the sides of the toilet I was seated on. Freddy had unbuttoned my police uniform shirt, exposing my big muscular chest, big pecs and fleshy nipples. In the side of my mouth a stinky cigar smoldered, Freddy's instructions for me to keep the thing wedged there, telling me that when he came back if the cigar wasn't in my craw he would make me sorrier than I already was. The smoke from the damned thing wafted upwards, assaulted my nostrils and irritated the fuck out of my eyes, making them tear. I puffed on the thing as ashes from it fell to my stretched out under shorts around my ankles.

"Freddy!" I seethed stupidly with the cigar dangling out of the side of my mouth. "Don't fucking leave me in here like this!"

"Relax dumb cop, I'll be back for you soon," Freddy said teasingly. "And by then you should be pretty well chewed up and eaten."

He left, closing the door behind himself.

"Damn it!" I roared. *"Damn it all!"*

It didn't take long before someone came into the men's room, namely the guy who was dressed as a marine. Smiling meanly, he slowly entered the stall.

"Fuck it all man, check out the hunky and would be cop," he cackled snidely. "Fuckin' handcuffed, tied up, stripped of your goddamned pants and sittin' on a toilet in your damned socks and shoes with your under shorts down around your ankles and smoking a stinking stogie. What a stooge you look like man!"

"I am no would be cop," I ranted as he entered the stall. *"I am a New York City police officer!"*

"Yeah, and if that's the case, if your cop buddies could see you now," the guy said mockingly.

"Fucker," I razzed him.

"Man oh man, I got to say, your tits look delicious cop," he said to me, looming over me, looking hungrily and lustfully at my big chest.

"And this time you got your uniform shirt wide open eh?" he asked me. "Looks to me like you're really asking for the treatment in here."

For a second he took the cigar from my mouth, helped himself to a few puffs of it and then slid it back into my craw. Then, before I could react to his comment and what he had just done he slowly squatted beside me, leaned forward and his mouth landed on one of my exposed man tits, one of his hands gripping my socked calf tightly.

"Ohhhhh gods!" I roared as he violently sucked and slurped my man tit. *"Shit!"*

Holding my socked calf tight he lifted my tied foot slightly, pulling it up to my toes. I gyrated stupidly on that damned toilet as the guy dressed as a marine slurped harder at my man tit like crazy. My dick betrayed me again, getting hard and jutting straight up between my spread legs, my big juicy and wounded balls resting and throbbing on the closed toilet seat.

"Oh yeah, fucking A!" the guy dressed as a marine said when he stopped working the fuck out of my man tit.

"Please untie me man...*ullpppp!*" I said stupidly as his mouth landed on my other man tit.

I squirmed in a mixture of ecstasy and humiliation as I said on that toilet seat having my tits eaten by a faggot dressed as a marine. Fucking guy ran his hand up my tall sock and snapped the elastic in it as he slurped heartily at my man tits alternately. The smoke from the rancid cigar in my mouth was more than irritating my eyes at that point. I puffed it like crazy, trying to keep the smoke from driving me crazy. All I got for my trouble though was that puffing on that stogie made my head spin, or could it have been the guy sucking my man tits causing that? When he was done working the fuck out of my nipples they were red, raw, swollen to the size of two ripe cherries and pointing straight out...more than very erect. I had never seen them looking like that before, only because none of the girls I had dated had ever worked them like that before. My man tits were literally alive and tingling with a life of their own on my big chest. The guy let go of my calf and I was able to lower my foot back to flat on the floor. Standing up now, the guy dressed as a marine looked at me fiendishly as he slowly unzipped his pants. He took his hard dick out of his uniform pants and holding it in one hand squatted down in front of me this time and brazenly took my dick in his other hand.

"Oh gods, what now?" I asked him.

In response he began stroking his dick and mine, stroking his manhood in and out of his foreskin. The last time I'd seen a guy with a thick foreskin was back in my police rookie days. Watching this guy now stroking himself in and out of his foreskin, squatting in front of me, stroking me at the same time brought back the memory of pissing beside the rookie in the men's room back in my police training days. Fuckin' rookie dude used to love stroking himself in and out of his foreskin while he pissed, putting on a good show for anyone who happened to be standing beside him at the urinals. But then, the sensations of having my sore dick stroked cut the memory short. The guy dressed as a marine stroked me faster and I realized that I was going to shoot a fourth fucking load. He was breathless and panting as he stroked himself in and out of his foreskin, squeezing my cop cock good and hard. Looking at my cock as it throbbed in his hand he shot his load first, into his hand.

"Oh yeah! Yeah Cop yeah! Seeing you all trapped and tied like this really gets me the fuck off," he panted in total ecstasy.

"Fucking pervert, goddamned pansy ass faggot done up like a marine," I seethed at him as he stroked his mess from himself, the smoke from the cigar wedged in my craw again irritating the fuck out of my eyes. "Let go of my cop cock you bastard!"

It seemed that all my ranting, insults of him and my bound up situation spurred the guy on even more. Then, using his mess of cum as a lubricant he stroked my pulsing and sore meaty dick faster and faster.

"Ohhhhhrrrrr god, you pervert, you fucker," I ranted, the ashes from the cigar wafting down onto my chest.

Once again my feet were raised to my toes as I sat there being jacked off like some cheap whore, gyrating myself stupidly on that damned toilet. The guy stroked me even faster and harder, squeezing the fuck out of my poor cop cock. Finally, I shot a fourth load.

"Oh yeahhhhhrrrrr!" I groaned like a banshee as I spurted small thick ropes of cop cum from my dick into his hand, mixing my load with his. "Yeah!"

I shot my load more and more into his hand and he smeared his cum and mine all over my cigar ash messed up chest, rubbing our thick soup mostly into my sore nipples.

"Please untie me now man…" I whimpered breathlessly, lowering my tied feet flat to the floor again.

He simply smiled at me, stood up, packed his spent manhood back into his pants and left the bathroom.

"Shit, *shit!*" I roared around the cigar wedged in my mouth. "Freddy, I will get you for this! For all of this! *Damn it!*"

As I sat there swearing the bathroom door opened and two rugged looking men dressed in black leather walked in. They found their way to the stall I was in and looked at me smugly.

"Well, well, well, the marine was right," the first leatherman said. "There really is a hot cop tied the fuck up in here."

They were both tall and from the way they filled out their leather tee shirts I could tell they were rock hard and muscular. I sat there feeling totally ridiculous as they moved into the stall at my sides. They smelled of a leather and sweat mixture.

"That marine was no marine!" I said through clenched teeth, the cigar halfway smoked down hanging out of the side of my mouth. "*But I am a real fucking and bad ass cop! I've been kidnapped!* And if you two leather pansies are smart you'll untie my damned feet and get these handcuffs off me!"

"Larry, get down there and suck this so called cops dick while I work on his beefy chest," the first leatherman said to the other.

The leatherman named Larry kneeled down in front of me, slurped my now aching dick into his mouth, and wrapped his hands around my socked calves. He began sucking me hard as his buddy slapped my pecs and chest hard, over and over, the stinging sounds echoing in the men's room.

"B-bastards! OWWWW!" I yelled. "Fuck it all, I'm going to add you guys to my arrest list when I'm out of this!"

"Some fucking cop," the first leatherman said mockingly. "No real cop would allow himself to be put into a position like this! Look at you with your goddamned under shorts down around your ankles."

I looked up at him angrily and then looked down to watch as his buddy sucked the fuck out of my big aching dick.

"Fucking guys," I ranted as I was sucked and meanly chest slapped real hard. "My cock is more spent than a maxed out credit card!"

"Then this should help you along Cop," the first leatherman said snidely and took the cigar out of my mouth.

He puffed my cigar and then with one hand forced my mouth wide open.

"UUUUHHRRRR, whaaaa…" I blanched and then looking downward as best I could I saw the fucker produce a tiny blue pill in his other hand.

"Eat this Cop," he said and dropped the pill in my mouth.

"H-HEY!" I ranted and before I could even think to spit the pill out he clamped my mouth shut and jerked my head back violently.

I felt the pill slide down my throat…

"FUCKER, what was that shit, some illegal street drug?" I seethed as the leatherman slipped my cigar back into my craw.

"NAW, nothin' like that Cop, just some Viagra mixed with a potent Chinese aphrodisiac," the leatherman snorted and slapped my pecs hard, the sounds of the slaps resounding in the stall of the men's room. "Freddy thought you might need some assistance to move you along while my boy here sucks you…"

And suck me he did, it seemed the guy was simply in love with my cop sized cock as he chowed down on it greedily.

"That pill should kick in pretty soon Cop," the leatherman said as his so called boy sucked me harder and harder and he squeezed and manhandled my fleshy tits. "Until it does my buddy and I will keep you good and worked up…HA!"

The guy's hands were caressing my blue socks and black shoes as he sucked me closer and closer to yet another cop gusher. Within a few minutes that pill I had been forced to swallow was working its sexual magic on me. I was breathless, to say the least. My pecs and chest as I saw, were turning a beet red color as the first leatherman relentlessly smacked and fuck, even punched them harder and harder. He squeezed and teased my poor nipples; really getting them worked up and beyond sore.

"Fuckers," I whispered miserably. "No way to be treating an officer of the law."

When I shot my Viagra induced load the leatherman sucking me swallowed the small spurt.

"Fucking pervert, eating my cop slop," I ranted crazily as the guy sucked down my juices, teasing the fuck out of my very sensitive manhood.

After I caught my breath, again, the leathermen left me alone in the men's room. What a mess I was and how fucking sick at heart I felt at that moment. I puffed on the cigar as the ashes fell from the front of it and landed at my feet and in my pulled down under shorts.

About five minutes past and then Freddy came into the men's room, followed by the muscular black bartender. Freddy locked the door behind them and they walked over to the stall I was in. In his hand Freddy was holding a glass filled to the rim with piss. The bartender was holding a camera. I gulped harder in horror more at the sight of that camera than at the glass of piss Freddy was holding.

"Hey there dumb cop," Freddy snickered, coming into the stall and standing over me at my side. "Enjoying yourself? Having a good time tonight?"

"F-Freddy, I'm no dumb cop man," I said angrily, looking up at him. "I swear to God, you're going to pay for this, *for all of it.*"

Freddy took the cigar from my mouth, slipped into his mouth and let it dangle there. Then, he placed one hand behind my neck and held the glass of piss to my trembling lips.

"Down the hatch Officer Stupid Smith," he said and fed me the rancid and sour tasting piss.

With no choice whatsoever in the matter I sipped down Freddy's piss, grimacing miserably every time I swallowed. As I drank piss the burly black bartender started snapping pictures of Freddy and me in the stall.

"Wh-whass tha-that guy doin'?" I gurgled in between sips of piss.

"Just what I told him to do Cop, he's taking pictures for the purposes of insurance," Freddy said meanly and force-fed me more piss.

When the glass was empty Freddy stuck what was left of the cigar in my mouth and stepped over to the bartender.

"Okay, lets get a few of him alone on the crapper," Freddy said, laughing as the bartender snapped a few pictures of me staring angrily straight ahead.

"F-Freddy, I want that camera," I stated with the utmost authority, my mouth a horrid taste of piss and cheap cigar. "Fuck man, now this is really taking things too far! FUCK!"

I struggled angrily as flash after flash from the camera exploded in my face.

"Man, if your cop buddies ever saw these pictures you would be drummed right off the force Officer," the bartender laughed as he snapped pictures of me. "Smile real pretty now."

"Fucker!" I ranted at him as the smoke from the cigar wafted up and irritated my eyes, making them tear.

When other guys came into the men's room Freddy invited them to pose for pictures with the "cop on the crapper" as he was entitling the roll of film. Two men in leather stood at my sides with their big meat sticks hanging freely by my face as pictures were taken. One mean guy reached down and grabbed one of my man tits and pulled hard on it, really stretching the beef of it as pictures were taken. My face contorted in agony and my dick betrayed me by getting hard for more of the pictures as the guy manhandled my man tit. It looked to me like that Viagra I had been force-fed was still working its magic on me. God, what a fucked up night it really had turned out to be. For the last of the pictures Freddy took the cigar out of my mouth, like earlier ground it out on my badge and fed me what was left of the ashes and the wet paper.

"Ha, can't believe you got that dumb cop eating that stogie," the bartender laughed and snapped pictures of my face in misery as I chowed on the cigar.

"I don't like wasting a good cigar man, you know that," Freddy said, he and the bartender watching as I swallowed and grimaced. "Don't worry cop, we'll give you some of the pictures to keep as souvenirs of the great time you're having tonight."

Freddy and the bartender laughed meanly. A few minutes later the bartender was gone and Freddy and I were alone in the men's room. He untied my ankles, hauled me to my feet and pulled my under shorts back up for me.

"Freddy, I want that camera and I want *all* that film as well you fucker," I spat angrily at my brawny captor. "You can't be circulating those pictures of me like that around man."

"You do as you're told dumb cop and those pictures will stay real private," Freddy said, buttoning my uniform shirt up for me and tying my tie.

My dick throbbed long and hard in my under shorts.

"We're leaving," Freddy said.

As he finished redoing my tie for me I asked him if he was letting me go.

"Letting you go?" Freddy asked me, patting me on the cheek. "Officer Stupid Smith, the night is just getting started."

That said Freddy took me by the arm and hustled me quickly out of the men's room. He walked me slowly out of the bar amid the stares of the other patrons there, including the bartender whose camera I saw on a shelf behind the bar. I looked longingly at the camera as Freddy walked me out of the bar and over to his car.

"Wh-where the fuck are you planning on taking me now?" I asked nervously as he opened the trunk of his car.

"Dancing, Officer Stupid Smith, I'm taking you dancing," Freddy replied with a grin.

"Dancing? *Dancing???*" I asked him, sounding more shocked than angry at the fact that he still wasn't releasing me. "You have got to be joking!"

Suddenly, Freddy scooped me up off the ground like a bridegroom lifting his bride and spun me around a few times.

"You are going to have a grand fucking time Smith Cop!" he said, spinning me faster as he held me aloft, my legs stretched out long in front of me. "The boys where I'm bringing you next will love you!"

He spun me faster still.

"Strong guy you are fucker, *put me the fuck down man!*" I yelled. "Help,

help! Cop down!"

Freddy threw me bodily into the trunk of the car.

"HUUUHHHFFFFF!" I gasped as I hit the interior of the trunk real hard, my back and head taking most of the blow.

Freddy quickly stuffed a rag into my mouth, effectively gagging me.

"Stupid fucking cop!" he snarled at me. "Ain't no one around here to help you! *You are mine!"*

With that he slammed the trunk shut. I shuddered in a mixture of misery and fear as I heard Freddy get into the driver's seat and then the car was moving again through the dark, late night and deserted streets of New York City...

Later, Freddy parked his car in an alley behind a big dance club on the sleazy West Side. It was a raunchy gay dance place where the patrons had the option of checking most of or all of their clothes at the door. Freddy scooped me out of the trunk and looked me over. Needless to say I looked pretty sad and ridiculous for a New York City police officer in just my long navy blue socks, patent leather lace-up shoes, my sweaty and cigar ash stained under shorts and my uniform shirt and tie on. And not to mention the burnt ashes on my badge from the times Freddy had doused his cigar against it. My mouth was rancid with the tastes of cum, piss and cigar ashes.

"Let's go," Freddy said and took the gag out of my mouth, cramming it in his pocket.

At the door Freddy stripped his shirt off and walked me into the club, holding me tightly by the arm. The music was pulsing and loud out by the dance floor and I saw that most of the patrons of the place were very scantily dressed...I was the only poor slob with his hands cuffed behind himself. I noticed how the men were all checking out Freddy's bare massively muscled chest as we made our way through the place.

"You thirsty Smith Cop?" Freddy asked me loudly above the pulsing music.

"Yeah," I replied, knowing too well what he was going to give me to drink.

"I'll have a couple of beers and then I'll let you have my piss," Freddy said to me, his lips right up against my ear, his tongue teasing the inside of it.

More men were checking Freddy out as he made his way with me to the bar. At the bar my captor ordered a beer and I saw that even the bartender was looking hungrily at Freddy's chest. Somehow I felt a twang of jealousy. The bartender placed Freddy's beer on the bar in front of him. Freddy paid for the beer and the bartender again looked at him hungrily, practically drooling over the sight of Freddy's big nipples.

"Nice lookin' cop you have there," the bartender said to Freddy.

"Thanks," Freddy replied. "I uh, just met him tonight and we're out on our first date."

I looked at Freddy angrily and he gave my erect cop cock a squeeze through my under shorts.

"Right Smith?" he asked me, his hand still on my crotch, making me breathless. "Our first date..."

"Do you always keep him handcuffed?" the bartender asked Freddy slyly.

"For now yeah, I don't want him getting away from me and it reminds him of whose in charge!" Freddy said and took a long gulp of his beer.

The bartender then looked at me, smiled, and said "Lucky you!" I looked away from him in utter dismay, knowing that if I told him that I was a real cop who'd been abducted he would never believe me. Freddy took another long swallow of his beer.

"Listen," Freddy said to the bartender. "I want to explore the club for a while, if you know what the fuck I mean. Can you keep my cop here until I get back?"

"Sure thing my man," the bartender replied. "I have just the spot for him right here under the bar."

"Freddy, don't leave me here with this guy!" I seethed through clenched teeth. "You and I have a date down at the precinct man!"

"Man, he plays his part real well," the bartender said with a smile. "You've got him trained real well after only one date."

The bartender lifted up the section of the bar that allowed entrance and Freddy simply looked at me.

"Freddy please…" I pleaded.

"Move it Smith Cop!" Freddy said sternly, giving my ass a hard painful squeeze. "I'll be back for you soon!"

With people watching I walked miserably behind the bar and stood next to the lecherous bartender. He closed the entrance to the bar.

"Don't let him drink anything from the bar," Freddy said to the bartender.

"I've got him on a piss diet."

The bartender laughed and he and Freddy gave each other a high five. Freddy left the bar and the bartender, holding me by my upper biceps put me down under the bar in a kneeling position next to a small sink filled with empty glasses. I just made it to fit into the spot he installed me in actually. A few minutes passed, the bartender served some patrons some drinks and beers, and when it wasn't too busy at the bar he stood over me. Very discreetly, or maybe not too discreetly he slipped his dick out of the fly opening of his jeans and dangled it in front of my face. Even soft, it was big, fat and juicy looking. It twitched a few times with a life of it's own and I didn't need to be told once what the fuck to do. As the bartender leaned casually on the bar I sat up slightly higher on my knees and greedily slurped his sausage sized rod into my mouth and sucked it for all I was worth. I had no choice really. His dick tasted like sweat and piss mixed together, and the smell (unbelievably) was somehow turning me on big fucking time. My cop cock grew harder yet in my under shorts and pressed hard against the white cotton material. Fuck, I was ready to shoot yet another damned load of cop slop, if someone were to have assisted me that is. As the bartender stood there feeding me his dick no one at the bar seemed to know what was happening. His dick, hard as a rock now and pulsing in my mouth was throbbing like crazy, as I said, with a life of it's own, as I sucked it harder and harder…and harder still. All at once the bartender grunted and a big thick load of white creamy man juice erupted from his piss hole into my mouth. He forced his dick further still into my mouth. He seemed to cum and cum and forced me to swallow every damned drop of it. I chowed down on his jizz, gulping it down, as he seemed to endlessly fill my mouth with it.

"Heh, hope your master isn't too mad that I fed you my cum," the bartender said, the last droplets of his mess sliding down my throat. "Seeing as he has you on a piss diet and all that."

I looked up at him with his dick still filling my craw.

"But it'll be our little secret eh Cop?" he asked me, thrust a few times and unbelievably shot one last rope of cum into my mouth.

I grimaced miserably and scoffed it down.

When he was (finally) done he tucked his spent dick back into his jeans, zipped up and resumed serving customers at the bar. I of course stayed where I was, waiting for Freddy to return, licking the bartender's remaining cum from my lips. My cop cock throbbed painfully in my under shorts. As I knelt there under the bar Freddy was in the men's room having some fun of his own. He stood with his legs spread wide as two guys sucked his big brown nipples and a third guy was on his knees sucking Freddy's big dick, which was hanging out of his jeans.

"Oh yeah, cock and tit hungry bastards you guys are," Freddy grunted. "Suck me, suck me real good. *Work me the fuck over with those tongues!*"

All the guys ran their hands over Freddy's big arms, his butt cheeks and chest, adoring him, the man who had gotten the drop on me and taken me captive…the man who had made me drink his piss…the man who I would also come to adore. The three guys all took their turns on Freddy's nipples and dick. Finally, when he could hold it back no longer he shot his load and one of the cock hungry guys swallowed it all.

"Ohhhhrrrr yeah!" Freddy roared like a lion in heat. "Fucking A, yeah!"

A few minutes later Freddy returned to the bar to collect me.

"Hey, how's my cop doin'?" Freddy asked the bartender.

"Just fine," the bartender responded, handing Freddy another beer. "That ones on the house."

"Yeah thanks, I'm going to have to piss real soon," Freddy said jokingly.

Freddy chugged his beer and then told the bartender to get me out from under the bar. Freddy took me by my arm and walked me through the crowded dance club to the men's room…as at the leather bar earlier, I felt eyes staring at me and drinking in the sight of me as I walked beside Freddy. In the men's room the three guys who had sucked Freddy off earlier were now waiting for yours truly; captured and helpless Officer Smith.

"Gentlemen, I promised you a hot cop, and here he is!" Freddy said to the three young men. "I want all of you to work him hard and make him drink your piss. He loves it!"

At the sight of me all three of the men's eyes lit up big and bright. In seconds their hands were all over me, my tie was pulled off me and my uniform shirt was unbuttoned. Their big mangy hands roamed all over my muscular chest, pinched my nipples like crazy, and they took turns slapping my stomach real hard, the sound echoing loudly off the tile walls.

"Perverts, *goddamned sleazy faggots,*" I seethed angrily as they handled me like a sex toy of sorts.

One of the men knelt at my side and sniffed my musty under shorts as he ran his big hands over my socks and shoes. Freddy stood against a wall nearby watching the spectacle of me being pawed, a mocking look of satisfaction on his handsome face. I didn't know whether to love or hate him at that moment as my dick grew harder in my under shorts. The three men continued to paw and maul me like mad, really squeezing the fuck out of my nipples, slapping my rock hard six pack stomach harder and harder, and stealing sucks at my nipples as well. I swooned in the forced ecstasy, moaning and grunting like crazy, thinking what the fuck my cop buddies would think if they could see me now. The guy kneeling at my side was licking my goddamned under shorts, sniffing them, and squeezing my socked calves all at the same time.

"Oh yeah, hot fucking cop is right," the first guy said directly into my ear, giving my earlobe a quick nip, squeezing one of my nipples at the same time. "Going to make you drink my cum *and my piss!*"

Then, all three men had their hard, throbbing, pre cum oozing cocks out of their jeans. The guy kneeling on the floor was stroking himself, aiming his piss hole at my shoes and socks.

"Fucking faggots, perving all over me," I grunted through clenched teeth.

The other two men were stroking each other, their cocks aimed up at my chest. They planned to shoot their loads all over my muscular chest and nipples. (Or so I thought.) The guy on the floor sniffed heartily at my under shorts, continued stroking himself, and then shot his load all over my shoes and socks. God, as I said earlier, what a night it had turned out to be. Moments later I was on my knees, kneeling in the middle of the three men. The first two guys finally shot their loads, in my mouth, forcing me to swallow every damned drop of it. Then, all three of the men were ready to piss. I leaned back with my mouth wide open, ready to guzzle their piss, just wanting it to be over already.

"See?" Freddy asked them. "I told you he loves it."

One at a time the men fed me their piss, holding the tip of their dicks directly on my trembling lips. I swallowed every drop they fed me, not losing any of it. Then, when they were done they packed their rods back into their jeans and filed out of the men's room, thanking Freddy as they went. Slowly, as best a man could do with his hands cuffed behind him I pulled myself to my cum soaked feet. My shirt was still hanging open, exposing my sore, swollen, bit up and mauled nipples along with my well-smacked red-marked stomach. Freddy looked at me standing there in total and utter misery and slowly walked over to me.

"Freddy, please, *no more,*" I said breathlessly and pleadingly. "I-I've learned my lesson…"

Smiling, Freddy hooked his thumbs and first and second fingers tightly around my sore, aching nipples and squeezed them hard.

"Ahhhhhhhh, shit, easy with my poor man tits Freddy," I gasped as he twisted them.

"Tell me what I want to hear Cop," Freddy said sternly, squeezing my nipples harder still.

"I-I'm gay man," I panted, not believing my own ears as I said it. "I'm a fuckin' bad ass *gay cop…*"

Freddy let go of my nipples and looked at them fiendishly. They had been worked up to two rubbery looking points on my big chest.

"I'm getting a real nasty idea here Smith Cop," Freddy said and took my nametag off my uniform shirt.

"Ohhhhhh gods Freddy, no, *no,* not what I think you're going to do man," I pleaded, backing away from him and pressing myself helplessly up against the tile wall.

Freddy simply stepped forward and proceeded to pin my nametag onto my left nipple, piercing it…

"AYYYYRRRR *shit!*" I seethed angrily. "Damn it man, damn it all you bastard, *you pierced my man tit!*"

"Deal with it Cop, or I'll pin your badge to your other tit," Freddy threatened as I stood there squirming in misery. "Now, tell me again…"

"I-I'm gay Freddy," I sputtered. "Always was, always knew it too…I guess it just took this night and you to bring it out of me."

He took my face in his hands and kissed me on my cum, piss and cigar tasting lips.

"Let's get out of this club," Freddy said, jamming a fresh cigar in my mouth, lighting it and taking me by the arm.

A half-hour or so later Freddy and I were sitting on the bench in the park where all this had begun earlier that fateful night. My uniform pants were back on me, my shirt was neatly buttoned, and my nametag was back on my shirt, and I sat still as Freddy slowly knotted my tie around my neck. My badge was cleaned of the cigar ash, courtesy of Freddy making me lick it clean.

"Some night huh Cop?" Freddy asked me.

I managed a small smile and kissed Freddy on the lips.

"Shit Smith Cop, I didn't plan on having you fall in love with me," Freddy said as he put my gun belt around my waist. "What the fuck and I going to do with you now?"

"Well, you could start by taking these damned handcuffs off me," I replied. "And then maybe getting us something to eat, seeing as all I've chowed on tonight is cum, piss and cigar ash."

Freddy freed my hands and we hugged each other tight, neither of us wanting to let go.

"I loved you the minute I saw you Smith," Freddy whispered in my ear. "When you walked up to me I knew it."

"Me too fucker," I replied softly, my cop cock tingling in my pants at the thought of all that Freddy had subjected me to that night.

"From now on no more nights like this one," Freddy said to me with total authority. "The only man who can have you from now on is me."

I readily agreed. I had learned my lesson and came out of the closet all in one night. As I said earlier this story happened a couple of years ago. I'm still a bad ass cop but now Freddy and I live together and he keeps me strictly in line at home. I closed the photo album, leaned back in my chair, puffed my cigar and whispered, "Yup, life is good."

Men at Play
(The Garage - A Prelude)

Matt slowly walked into the dark deserted parking garage and found his driver, Rico, pissing in a corner. The handsome young executive stopped short and stood there in his expensive prissy suit and clothing, staring at Rico's cock with his beautiful mouth hanging opened, his tongue nearly dangling out of his mouth as well. Rico saw Matt standing there in all his suited glory and grinned fiendishly. He grabbed Matt roughly by the front of his thin cotton dress shirt and flung the executive against the wall.

"UHHHFFFF…" Matt grunted in total surprise, his driver treating him this way a total shock to the handsome executive.

As Rico flung him Matt heard the stitching in his expensive shirt rip.

"So, you like seeing a man's cock, don't you, you pretty fag, jeez, I been waiting for just the right moment to land your prissy and sexy ass," Rico intoned in his heavy Spanish street sounding accent. "Now, get down there and taste that big cock, seeing as you like it so much…"

As Matt tried to squirm away from his driver turned rapist Rico grabbed the executive's tie in his hugely muscular fist and dragged the cringing executive to his knees. As Matt's head spun Rico shoved his face into his crotch. The handsomer than handsome executive got a good hearty whiff of his driver's cock and balls through his uniform trousers, it was a strong musky funky male odor that was for sure. Rico knocked Matt down further to the grimy floor and kicked him in the ass, leaving a big dirty boot print on Matt's right butt cheek, really mussing up the pretty executive's suit trousers back there.

"Get the fuck down there and sniff the piss I pissed you faggot pretty boy, do it, in your perfect suit," Rico swore.

Shaking in disbelief at this rebellion of his driver Matt saw a big puddle of urine all foamy and yellow, still hot from Rico's cock all over the pavement he was lying on.

"Get in there pig boy, fucking prissy silk socked exec," Rico said meanly, roughing his boss up some more, slapping Matt hard all around.

Matt's expensive clothing was all disheveled now, getting dirtier as he was manhandled, getting torn. As Matt tried to make a move to defend himself Rico grabbed his employer's suit jacket and ripped the pocket off. Matt was flailing around, swearing and grunting in disbelief, making sounds like a fucking hog and one of his black laced up wingtip shoes came off his foot. Rico laughed, picked up the shined shoe and spit all over the stupid delicate leather. Then, he shoved the shoe in Matt's handsome face. Rico stepped with both feet in the puddle of urine and commanded Matt to kiss his tootsies. When Matt looked up at the driver in total bewilderment Rico shoved his foot down. All Matt saw was his driver's hard leather dress boots and all he smelled was the sharp scent of the man's piss. Grabbing Matt by the back of his head and twining his fingers in his wavy hair Rico pushed Matt down until his mouth was right on the smelly urine. As his head was forced downward Matt could not resist. He felt the piss and dirty rough leather on his lips now and he tasted it. Rico then flipped Matt on his back and proceeded to wipe his filthy piss stained boots on him, degrading the poor guy more and more.

"I will use you like a floor mat," Rico ranted, wiping the wet dirty soles of his boots on the front of Matt's silk tie, his white fine cotton shirt and all over his suit jacket and suit trousers.

Matt squirmed miserably under the driver's stance, his beautiful suit being ruined, ruined, ruined…

Rico still had his dick and balls out and Matt could see how meaty, beefy and hard the driver's manhood was. His balls were hanging down, swinging back and forth; his cock was powerful and menacing looking. With a quick easy motion Rico reached down and ripped open Matt's suit trousers, pulling them down to his black sheer nylon over the calf socks and gartered ankles.

"Well, ain't that just too sweet, fucking prissy sheer socks *and* garters, how dapper, how spiffy indeed," Rico said mockingly as he held the tatters of Matt's suit pants in hand, standing over the terrified executive. "You must have lived a past life or two in the roaring fucking twenties huh my silk socked exec?"

Then, Rico took a look at Matt's tight nylon bikini briefs and decided he needed to get his ass pissed on and whipped. He hauled Matt up by the shoulders and as the executive made a move to resist Rico shoved the perfect handsome face against the wall. Matt started to cry at that point. Rico got a grip on Matt's shirt tails and the hem of his suit jacket and pulled it up to the back of his neck, ripping it almost in half. He ripped off Matt's black silk undershirt and started meanly slapping the executive's naked back. Matt howled in a mixture of pain and anger at this awful, awful violation. The young executive still could not believe how his driver had turned against him.

Then, Rico leaned on Matt, holding him against the wall, gripping his tattered clothing. He started spanking and pissing on Matt's ass through his flimsy black nylon briefs. It hurt like hell being spanked that way but Matt felt himself getting a major hard cock. Rico's hard masculine hands' slapping his helpless ass with muscular force was unnerving for Matt, yet so arousing somehow. Matt yelped and tried to hop around, his legs flailing. The garters on his socks snapped loose from all the struggling he was doing and the executive's sheer nylon socks fell down to his ankles.

"Yes, dance for me pretty boy fag," Rico ordered as Matt hopped and hobbled. "I've got you standing in that puddle of my stinking piss. Your one sheer nylon over the calf prissy sheer sock is soaked through and your other shoe is getting a good thorough dousing with male urine."

Matt could feel it soaking inside. He then heard (and felt) the hard sharp cracking sound of Rico's hand meanly beating his sexy ass. The executive's clothing was filthy and stinking from Rico's piss. Matt hopped around in the piss, swinging his great ass and splashing Rico's piss all over his suit trousers. The executive's faggot ass cheeks were throbbing when Rico finally stopped spanking him. As Matt stood there panting and crying Rico pulled Matt's nylon briefs down and saw a cum stain on them.

"You fucking pretty boy faggot, you like all this shit don't you?" Rico teased his employer.

Matt reluctantly nodded "yes."

Rico then threw Matt on the hood of the car, the executive landing with a "HOOOF" sort of sound escaping him. Matt felt Rico's hard body, muscular and tight, lean on him. Rico's manly groin pressed hard against Matt's delectable ass cheeks. Matt then felt Rico's hard dick head rubbing against his asshole, heard his deep manly breathing. Suddenly, Matt felt a tremendous violation of his body as Rico shoved his hard cock inside, penetrating Matt's tight asshole. Matt felt that hard muscular force go all the way into the deepest part of his gut. He was totally violated. His guts felt completely filled. The executive was moaning like a fucking animal. Rico started fucking Matt then, big time, his huge cock going in and out of his beautiful tight ass-cunt, fucking him over and over. Moans and guttural sobs were keening from Matt's hot mouth. Rico fucked and fucked Matt a long time, deep and very thoroughly. When Matt thought he would not be able to endure anymore Rico shot a wad of sticky slimy hot white cum way up inside him. It made Matt's ass feel fully open and wide. Rico pulled his cock out of Matt's hole slowly, very slowly. As he did so Matt himself shot a load with such force that the executive thought he was going to faint, shaking, and his knees gave way. Matt fell to the floor on his knees. Rico's cock was still hard and Matt saw that the big knobby dick head and shaft were slimy with his ass juices and from being fucked in his male ass-cunt. Rico placed his twitching cock on his employer's lips. This was a moment to remember…

Matt could see that Rico had torn off his sheer black nylon over the calf sock and garter and was holding them in his hand. He leaned his manly crotch closer toward Matt's face.

"You can't stop looking at my ass fucking dick can you?" he barked and Matt felt his mouth drop open.

The executive of such stature and standing could not believe he was doing this. Matt let his jaw fall open and Rico shoved his ass juice covered cock into his mouth.

"FUCK, I've got you totally degraded now, pretty man/boy, ass fucked pussy executive," Rico swore as Matt gobbled on his cock. "Take my man-cock in your perfect mouth. I'm going to wipe all my juice and piss all over the inside of your mouth. FUCK, I'm going to take a piss, take a long piss fully in your mouth."

Rico smiled wickedly at Matt who looked up at him with THOSE HAUNTING BROWN EYES. Rico pulled his dick out of his employer's mouth and finished pissing all over Matt's ripped and very soiled clothing. He also pissed on his black laced shoes and sheer nylon socks and garters. Rico then stuffed the ruined sheer black sock in Matt's opened mouth and wrapped the garter roughly around his head, tying the garter tightly, gagging Matt with the piss stained sheer sock…

Matt watched Rico get into his big truck and the guy grabbed a beer out of the cooler. Gagged with his own smelly sheer sock and the sock tied into his mouth with the garter Matt did not dare make a move. He was too beaten to shit at that point to try anything against the man he employed.

"I'm not done with you yet," Rico snarled, holding the beer in hand. "There's going to be a lot more piss and cum, and I'm going to fuck you harder and longer, I am going to fuck the shit out of your perfect tight ass-cunt and defile your suit and tie and the rest of your clothing with it."

Finally, Matt smiled, for in reality he was a happy man. He had finally met A MAN he could relate to. He did have a position opened after all…

Matt's Driver

Matt's hugely muscular and hard-bodied driver Rico has forced the handsome executive to buy him fine dress clothes, which will complement his chauffeur's uniform right nicely Rico thought snidely. Now he comes to Matt's office whenever he feels like it, even if the executive is busy as hell, and fucks his ass on an almost daily basis. His strong masculine body looks hard and dangerous at the same time in his exquisitely tailored suits. Matt recalled taking his driver for fittings and try-ons in a men's haberdashery store recently. While Rico stood tall and at attention on a square box while the tailor of the store made the necessary alterations on one of the suits he was buying for him Rico smiled fiendishly over at his employer. Matt's asshole twitched at that look and he knew he should fire the fucking guy for what he had done to him in the garage that day…but at the same time his cock grew stiff in his own suit pants as Rico smiled at him in a lecherous way. Matt had come to wonder who the boss and who the employee was at this point. When he comes to Matt's office Matt automatically stands up at the sight of him. He pulls on his suit jacket knowing the madness he is in for as Rico places his huge manly hands all over the young and handsome executive, defiantly rumpling his clothes as he does so. Rico meanly squeezes the lapels of Matt's suit jacket, creasing them. He tugs on Matt's tie, making it all askew. As he slams the executive against a wall he kisses Matt hard and long and rough on the mouth, slurps Matt's tongue into his craw and sucks it till the executive thinks he is going to bight his tongue right out of his mouth. As he leans against the wall in a mixture of torment and ecstasy Matt pulls himself to his wingtip tiptoes. When the door to Matt's office is locked a few moments later Rico forces his employer to take off his shoes and suit pants. Matt stands there in his sheer nylon socks and tight garters, his personal favorites, with his soft silky boxer shorts pulled down.

Sometimes Rico wraps Matt's shirttails around one fist so he can hold the executive down while he spanks his tender white ass cheeks. After that's done and he is gone Matt will think of Rico all day while he sits. He will think of him and wonder what sort of nastiness he has awaiting him for the end of the day when he gets in his car to be driven home. Rico's big workman's hand is hard as a wooden plank and the pain is intense as he spanks his boss. Matt struggles to keep from crying out, hoping that no one, "NO ONE" outside the locked office can hear the sharp crack of Rico's hand on his poor pathetic ass cheeks. The driver knows Matt cannot resist him and he intends to spank the executive with full brutal force. Being dressed as an executive himself and not a driver in a chauffeur's uniform gets Rico into Matt's office all the more easily. He hits Matt slowly at first, each blow is a sharp cutting surprise of pain, and then with hard rapid strokes that blend together into an unbearable hot burning pressure on Matt's ass.

Rico sees the tears running down Matt's beautifully handsome face and chuckles meanly in satisfaction. Matt cannot believe how strong the man is, and he cannot believe how the tables have been so brutally turned in their stations to each other. The executive finds himself bent over his desk with Rico leaning on his back while he delivers what seems like an endless violent assault on his naked helpless ass. Matt finally gasps out loud, so Rico shoves one of his wingtips deep into the executive's mouth. Matt looks back at the man in disbelief. "Gagged with a goddamned shoe?" his eyes seem to be saying angrily. He cannot help it though as he bights down on it when Rico goes back to beating his ass with renewed manly vigor. Matt finds that the man is strong enough to beat on him until he is completely humiliated, and then some. Matt's cock tingles long and hard in front of him. Matt flails his legs to try to get away from the ongoing spanking assault but his sheer nylon socks just slide pitifully on the plush carpet of his office. The executive realizes he cannot escape this degrading abuse.

Matt finally slumps to the floor in a daze at his driver's feet. This is worse than all the times that Rico has come to his office. He has really worked him over big time this time. Rico then shoves Matt down even further and the executive realizes he has no choice but to kiss and lick the driver's fine shoes, shoes that he himself paid for. As Matt licks Rico's shoes he thinks how once he has been sent to the floor he is to lick his shoes, Rico's orders at the beginning of his training as he called it. Matt recalled how Rico had held him by a handful of his wavy hair and snarled at him that in the office he was the boss, but once he was present all bets were off. Rico had practically lifted Matt off the floor by his hair that time and when the handsome executive screamed in pain Rico punished him by fucking his ass hard with no lube for what seemed like hours. When he had thrown Matt to the floor before stripping him for the ass pounding he had ordered him to pay homage to his shoes with his tongue. As Matt did as he was told Rico told him how from now on when he was on the floor he was to lick his shoes…and then some. So now, as Matt did Rico's shoe licking bidding he looked up and saw that his driver had opened his suit pants and had pulled out his cock and balls. The effect of his huge manly genitals being revealed and framed by that dark elegant suit was especially obscene and threatening somehow to Matt. Rico leaned down and ripped off one of Matt's socks, stuffed it in his mouth and tied the young executive's garter around his head like a gag. Matt could never get used to being gagged with his socks, it sucked.

Rico then hauled Matt back up and over to his desk again. He kicked Matt's legs apart and pinned his muscular arms behind his back. In his other hand he had his huge and powerful mammoth sized cock.

"Beating you has gotten me all aroused and hard pussy boy," Rico seethed in Matt's ear. "Man, I am so ready to fuck the tar out of you."

Rico slid his thick ample foreskin back; his hard bulbous dick head was all wet and slimy with pre cum. He would be able to penetrate Matts' asshole no matter how much the executive tried to resist. Actually, he hoped Matt would resist. He liked it so much better that way. Matt panted and his ass clenched tight in fear but for some reason he leaned forward and Rico's dick head slowly punched through and his massive thick shaft slid up inside. When he entered Matt's ass hot waves of naked shame penetrated the executive's body.

He fucked Matt slowly, so slowly so he would feel each deep muscular thrust's maximum effect. Rico fucked Matt like an expert, holding him down and moving just his meaty thighs. The driver's huge dick violated his employer's asshole, going in deep, a pause, and out again, over and over and over. It was very quiet after that violent beating, just Rico's deep manly breathing and Matt's painful gasps as the driver's cock went in deeper and more forcefully each time.

Rico was really screwing Matt now and he knew that he owned the worthless faggot assed executive and that he could make the guy do anything he wanted. Just the fact that Matt had purchased all the fine clothing for him proved that. Rico was flexing every muscle in his manly body to work his cock in Matt's asshole. The driver was satisfied that he had fucked his boss thoroughly and now he was going to deliver some more punishment. Rico got a good grip on Matt and started to pound his body into the poor executive's ass. Matt now felt how strong his driver really was. All those workouts at the gym had really paid off for the guy it seemed, workouts and a gym membership that Matt paid for every month it should be mentioned. Rico was using the full weight of his massively muscular body and all of his manly strength to fuck and fuck Matt. His cock was ripping in and out of Matt's ass. His groin slammed against Matt's sore ass cheeks, making them burn like another spanking. Rico humped Matt, reamed out his asshole with his hard throbbing raw dick. The pressure in Matt's ass was making him squirm and moan. The executive's face was red and with the sock in his mouth he was panting through his nose like a stuck pig.

Rico's assault on Matt's ass was thorough and brutally relentless. Matt was amazed to see how fast a big muscular man like him could move. The driver's dick was a hard purple blur going in and out of his helpless and ruined asshole. The handsome executive felt as if his driver's penis had entered every part of his body. Rico gave a final massive thrust, shoved his cock in to the hilt and held it there, making Matt shudder as he was filled to overflowing in his asshole. The driver's huge knob-head was in Matt's guts it felt like. Matt knew that Rico was ready for a hard and violent climax. He felt the hot streams of cum pumping in his gut from the driver's throbbing penis. Thrust after hard thrust, a dozen wads of semen got pumped inside the handsome executive. Rico came very hard indeed, punching Matt's sopped hole with his manhood savagely for a long while.

Then, Rico allowed his cock to slide out of Matt's hole, slick with cum and butt slime. The executive crumpled to the floor again. Rico was satisfied, but still not done tormenting his employer. His cock was still hard and he wanted to make Matt worship it, and taste it. He knew inwardly how much his employer loved these sadistic scenes. He stepped over Matt as the guy lay on the floor heaving and sat down in his armchair.

Rico sat back in Matt's desk chair. He looked elegant and masculine with his clothes casually loosened. He had his feet out and spread wide apart, showing off his manly muscular legs. His dick was at the center, hard and sticking out rudely, ready again to dominate and abuse Matt further. Reaching down he grabbed Matt, took the sock and garter out of his mouth and dragged the poor guy into his crotch and put his face on his penis. Matt smelled the manly odor of his driver's genitals and the salty sweat in his groin. It was strong and pungent and yes, masculine.

Rico spit a few times onto his genitals and made Matt sniff and then lick his filthy cock. Matt could taste his own ass chowder on his driver's manhood. First Rico's knobby dickhead then he licked all the way down the thick hard meaty shaft to his driver's huge and bloated ball sac. He made Matt put his mouth on them, his lips, his tongue, every crevice and curve of his huge genitals. Matt tasted Rico's semen and the slime from his asshole left on Rico's cock. He felt it in his mouth and on his face. Then, he sucked his driver's cock, felt it sliding in and out of his mouth, a huge massive violation of his handsome puss.

As Matt chowed down on Rico's cock and the treats all over it the driver pulled him of by a handful of his hair and made the executive kiss and lick his ball sac some more.

"Yeah, I love that you pussy boy, lick my balls," Rico swore meanly.

Matt felt Rico spread his legs a little wider. With his hand on top of Matt's head Rico pushed him down a little more. The executive found that now his face was buried behind Rico's balls, in the darkest most private place on his body. The musky smell was overwhelming. Rico held Matt there for a long time, really making the guy smell that funky male odor, making him breathe it in. As Matt tried to pull away he felt that Rico had both his hands on his head now, holding him firmly in place. Matt then felt Rico's body shift, the muscles in his manly legs were now all around him. Rico grinned down as he now had his employer in just the right position; he had his fucking faggot mouth right at his filthy sweaty asshole. Somehow during this assault Rico had managed to get his suit pants down around his ankles along with his silk underpants. He slapped Matt's head and ordered him inside. As Matt lapped and did as he was told Rico swore at him like a marine drill sergeant, telling him to get his mouth in there and kiss his ass, and to lick that slimy and filthy asshole.

Matt felt an overpowering force inside his head making him open his mouth. Rico pushed forward and shoved hard. Matt felt his raw naked male asshole on his mouth. His lips were in full contact with his driver's bunghole. He could feel how smooth and muscular Rico's hole was, wet and pulsing around his tongue. YUCK! But Matt chowed down anyway. The slime was in Matt's mouth as he started to lick it, working his lips on it now. He opened his mouth wider to get the mans' ass in his mouth as Rico forced it on him.

"Suck it, yeah, you are now sucking your driver's ass," Rico swooned meanly, him becoming completely aroused now.

Rico stood up and shoved his hard throbbing cock in Matt's mouth. It was still wet and slimy from having had Matt suck him. He held Matt's head by the ears and face fucked him brutally. Matt was by now gagging and about ready to puke, but Rico had him in just the right position so he could penetrate his boss's throat and completely face fuck him. He was fucking Matt's face just the way he knew the boss liked it and now he was going to make him eat his cum. Rico had a hard and brutal climax. As he did so he grabbed Matt by the throat and the back of his head and held him tight as his dick spurted its deposit down his throat. Huge wads of semen spiraled and shot around in Matt's mouth. It felt all gooey and slimy on his tongue but he forced it down anyway even as Rico went on thrusting in his craw. Matt's throat then had a tight astringent feel when Rico's dick made him swallow convulsively.

When he was done Rico ripped Matt's silky boxer shorts off him and cleaned himself up with them…

Matt was too exhausted to get up off the floor. He could see that Rico was very satisfied and very happy now that he had completely abused and humiliated his boss. He had beat Matt into submission, then had fucked his ass, then fucked his mouth and made him service his raunchy asshole. Rico chuckled as he thought of his boss man eating his semen and eating his ass with his mouth.

"You will taste it and feel it in your ass for the rest of the day till I drive you home tonight," Rico said snidely and before he left he took a piss in Matt's other shoe.

Matt barely managed to get himself together enough during the day to go home. He knew that the chauffeur would be back to use him again, perhaps to even abuse him when he reached home that night…

That night Matt told Rico that he was leaving for a business trip, he thinking that he would be spared his hard use for a while, but Rico informed Matt that he had other plans for him…and that he would be coming along on the trip…an executive needs his driver after all…

Matt's Driver

Part Two

Matt's driver, Rico, had been savagely fucking the young handsome executive two or three times a week now for several months. Sometimes he would throw in a day or two extra just to keep his handsome employer on his toes. On his toes, Rico had to laugh at that, seeing as the last time he had fucked Matt's asshole that's where the executive stood, on his sheer socked toes, impaled on Rico's huge crust as he thrust in and out of him mega-savagely. Matt never knew when to expect him to show up for an abusive fuck session. It could be at any moment that he would arrive Matt had learned. The driver was always clad in the exquisitely tailored suits and perfect shoes and silk underwear and sheer black nylon over the calf hosiery and garters along with the power ties that he made his boss buy for him. Rico had come to love this twisted arrangement. As the driver he was Matt's employee, but when it came to sexing the executive down Rico found he enjoyed being the boss. He wore the fine clothes with such casual masculine elegance that no one would suspect that he brutally dominated Matt with his body constantly, and that he raped his boss with such violent athletic skill. Somehow, somewhere deep inside his most secret self Rico knew that Matt craved this sort of treatment. The fact that Matt had not fired his driver attested to that. Rico's control over Matt was complete at that point in the sexual arena and he made the man submit to every aspect of his manhood. And Matt knew what Rico's body was like under that perfectly fitted silk undershirt and jacket. The driver's muscles were hard, crude and masculine. He never hesitated to beat and torture the handsome executive...to brutally force Matt's body to his will, or just for the pleasure of making him take it. Matt was always surprised at how ferociously Rico assaulted him, physically, mentally and sexually. But Matt could not deny either the wave of fear and admiration he felt for Rico's manhood when he became aroused and came for him, revealing his manly body and powerful genitals. Every time Rico took Matt he fucked the executive's tight ass harder, longer and more thoroughly. He degraded Matt and his expensive clothes more and more completely. While half stripped, while wearing just his sheer socks, while wearing nothing more than torn up silk underpants Matt is made to service Rico's manhood in degrading and most humiliating ways. Rico even forces Matt to breathe the male odor from every intimate part of his body, his asshole, his balls, and the space in between them. He has forced Matt to slurp, suck and lick the stink from his hairy armpits. Matt has taken huge amounts of Rico's semen into his body. He has tasted it in his mouth and had Rico ejaculate hard and deep inside his ass in long violent dominating male orgasms...

Now Matt was on a business trip headed for a remote city in South America. He had had his secretary make all the travel arrangements and took an earlier flight. He wanted to get there ahead of Rico, knowing what the driver would have in mind for him no doubt, and he was also taking several days time beyond the few days needed for the business at hand. When Matt arrived at the airport he had a car take him to his hotel. It felt strange being in a car that Rico was not driving, but for the moment it also was a relief not to be raped while on the way to the hotel. But it was when he arrived in his hotel room all decked out in a new Zegna suit that he realized Rico had turned the tables on him. The man had arrived at the hotel a day earlier than his employer and was waiting for him with a spear-like hard-on. When he walked into his room Matt was grabbed by his shoulders and thrown bodily onto the king-sized luxurious bed. He hadn't been accompanied by a bellhop seeing as his luggage was also sent ahead and was waiting for him in his room. As Matt rolled over, taken completely by surprise Rico sat down on the bed and hauled his employer across his knees. Even though Matt was fully dressed in a fine suit, silk shirt, tie and sheer black nylon over the calf socks and garters and his best made shoes Rico had him with his head forced down and his suited ass up. Rico flipped back the back of Matt's suit jacket and with a knife sliced it up the center to the collar and proceeded to spank the executive. Matt was irate, as he had just purchased this damned suit. Oh yes, he was also irate at being spanked like a little kid by the man who worked for him. Matt's arms were pinned in front of him, no way of escaping the pain and humiliation. The executive's legs flailed around behind him uselessly, he could feel the tightness of the garters around his perfect calves. Rico was working up a manly sweat as he spanked his employer so he took off his suit jacket, loosened his tie and unbuttoned his shirt. He yanked Matt's head up by a handful of his wavy hair and wiped his face in his smelly armpits. Rico's male odor was so familiar to Matt at this point, smutty, powerful and intoxicating somehow. The smell from Rico's pits through his shirt was forcefully intrusive. He forced Matt to linger there, holding him tight, getting the scent on the executive's nose, on his face, most importantly inside his head. When he was satisfied that Matt had serviced his pits enough for the moment he threw the poor guy down back across his lap. He spanked Matt HARDER now; there were tears in his soulful eyes, running down Matt's perfectly beautiful face. Some have called Matt's face "The Face of The Century" and Rico would agree. Rico then ripped Matt's silk shirt up the back, pulled his silk tie off by the collar it lay under and used it as a bondage tool to control Matt's neck and head movements.

"Hope you brought more clothes for this trip Pussy boy, you'll need them," Rico teased as he twisted Matt's head around, using the man's tie as a leash of sorts.

He then tore the cuffs off Matt's shirt and with his knife sliced the sleeves up to Matt's shoulders. Matt screamed at the sight of the knife as it sliced his shirt. Grinning sadistically Rico knifed through to Matt's silk undershirt, exposing the executive's jutted up and hard nipples. As Matt was feeling terrified Rico sliced his belt off him and cut the seam in his suit trousers all the way down to his crotch. Then, the legs of his suit trousers were cut, each leg down to the cuffs, the executive's sheer black nylon over the calf socks and garters and his silk black boxer shorts were now in full view.

The executive's ripped suit and shirt were simply dangling on his great looking body. Matt's body, like Rico's was a masterpiece of nature and of the gym as well. As Matt lay there he realized that Rico had the entire night to abuse him, ten hours of degrading assault. He had arrived at the hotel at a time when there would be no meetings to attend, that is until the next morning. He knew that he would be licking Rico's musky foreskin, ripe and slimy since he hadn't bothered to bathe since the day before. His dickhead would be shiny and it would smell like a men's locker room. After spanking Matt hand-wise Rico slumped the executive on the floor in front of him and whipped his ass with a belt until his mouth dropped open. Matt voluntarily took Rico's big stinking dick into his helpless waiting mouth and sucked it, anything to avoid being belt-whipped anymore. Then, Rico lifted Matt and pinned him on the bed like a wrestler, with Matt now on his back and Rico's sweaty, hairy muscular chest pressed against his face. He pinned Matt's legs back and he squeezed his balls until the sheer socked executive moaned miserably. Then he spit downward, right in Matt's angelically perfect face. Matt squirmed and struggled now, but could not turn away as he was spit on over and over and over.

"See what kind of a lowlife Boy/Man executive slave you really are?" Rico taunted his employer. "Some topnotch exec you are…"

And he spit again in Matt's face…

Then, Rico shoved Matt to the floor and slapped his spit slimed face. He pointed his semi hard cock at Matt and humiliating, AWFUL for Matt, Rico pissed on his face and down his body, wetting the executive's silk black boxer shorts as his cock hung hard, hanging through the slit in the silk material. Matt was appalled yet aroused at the same fucking time. The piss ended up dripping down to Matt's garters and sheer black nylon over the calf socks. Rico snickered and lifted one of Matt's socked feet to his cock and dried the head of his penis on the sole of the executive's socked foot. Then, he hefted Matt up, twined his huge fingers in the executive's wavy hair and balanced him on his socked tiptoes.

"Going to fuck you now you pussy Man/Boy executive," Rico seethed in Matt's ear as with his other hand he sheered away the back of Matt's silk boxers, exposing his melon shaped ass globes. "And this time I'm not using any goddamned lube…the scum from my dickhead should be just enough…"

He forced Matt into a most vulnerable position; the scum from his dickhead, as he had so aptly called it moments ago was just enough slickness to force poor Matt's asshole to open widely and gaping for Rico's manly desire. Soon the driver's thick meaty shaft was wet with slime from Matt's sweaty and opened asshole. Matt no longer looked like the regal executive he had been when he had first entered his hotel room not all that long ago. After being fucked Matt knew he would be beat some more. GAWD, he wondered, how in the fuck will I be able to make that meeting tomorrow in the early morn? For the second round of thrusting in and out of Matt's asshole Rico tied the executive's sheer socked ankles with his necktie, balanced him now on his tied feet and plowed in and out of him again, bringing Matt down to further submissive degradation. Matt had not made a move as his driver tied his sheer socked ankles, rather the hard-on in the executive's torn up silk boxers seemed to throb all the more as he watched his ankles being bound, his toes twitching under his sheer socks. Matt stood balanced precariously as after Rico was done fucking him and filling his asshole yet again with what felt like gallons of spunk the man raised his strong muscular arms and whipped, slapped and spanked him all over his clothing destroyed, piss stained, semi naked hard cocked body. Matt made sounds of "HOOOOFFF" and "OOOOFFFF" as he did his best to stay balanced on his tied up feet as he was throttled from all sides it seemed… Matt found that there was no way to avoid the blows being rained on him from Rico's fists and hands, the man was too fast and he was too beat to shit at this point…

Then, using his knife again Rico cut off Matt's silk boxer shorts. That left the head spinning and wounded executive wearing nothing except his sheer black nylon over the calf socks and garters, them dripping with his piss. As Matt stood there on his tied feet taking in his stripped appearance, looking down at himself he was amazed when Rico's cock entered his asshole yet again, strong and hard and spearing. This time he fucked Matt slowly and thoroughly, totally absorbed in his own manhood and Matt felt as if he was simply there to be used and to receive his driver's maleness. The smell from Rico's cock would eventually fill the room, his sweating pits would again be in Matt's face and the executive knew that this unrelenting fuck would go on and on... At one point Rico wrapped his hugely muscular arms around Matt, lifted him a few inches off the floor and as his socked feet dangled Matt found himself hoisted and impaled on his driver's manhood.

"Fucker..." Matt whispered in anger and awe.

A short while later Matt was on his knees in front of Rico as the driver sat at the end of the king-sized luxurious bed. Rico ordered Matt to remove his fine shoes for him with his teeth. Matt managed to undo the laces of Rico's shoes with his front-most teeth. The smell from his driver's black nylon sheer socks was perfect. As Rico's shoes were removed he took a break and Matt knew that he would watch the driver admire his fine manly body in the mirror. Rico looked at himself in the mirror as if he were in love with himself. Matt fumed inwardly, seeing as that body was the result of daily workouts at a high-priced gym, the membership paid for by Matt himself. Snickering when he finally stepped away from the mirror Rico took a new pair of Matt's sheer over the calf length socks from his luggage and as the executive struggled to no avail he bound his hands behind him at the wrists...with the socks. Matt cursed and fumed...

Then, Rico threw Matt on the floor, bodily. He stood over his employer, his socked feet right by his head. Matt watched in terror as Rico placed his masculine sheer socked foot in his drooling mouth. Like Matt Rico was now naked except for his socks and garters. His magnificent muscular male body was now completely revealed to the throttled executive. Matt looked up at every muscle and Rico's cock and balls seemed gigantic from his vantage point down on the floor. Rico placed one socked foot on Matt's chest and the executive felt the weight of it as he started to squat down.

"NO, NO!" Matt protested feebly as he watched Rico's massive thighs flex and his cock and balls sway. The man looked and felt menacing and dangerous now. Rico lowered himself till his broad and muscular ass was right above Matt. The hapless executive knew what was coming now and what would be expected of him. He wanted to bolt but he could not even turn away from the impending bunghole slathering his face. Rico laughed and ordered Matt to open his mouth. The words penetrated Matt's brain and he felt himself opening his mouth as wide as he possibly could. As he did so Matt saw what a filthy pig Rico really was as he lowered his big muscular and stinking man's ass onto the executive's handsome face. Rico stroked his huge ass cheeks all over Matt's face; back and forth he rocked, and then slid his mangy ass crack into position, directly over Matt's mouth and nose. He let Matt take a good long look at it. Deep inside his hard muscular ass crack Matt saw his fully exposed and raunchy asshole. It looked totally obscene, pink and surrounded by brown and purple. Rico's asshole was damp and muscular as Matt found out as he breathed in his funky anal stink. Rico reached around and with his strong hand on Matt's head he held his boss in position to service his asshole…and Matt did it. The executive's lips touched Rico's funky wet hole and he worked his mouth on it like his life depended on it. He could not believe how hungrily he went at it, not just licking it and kissing it here and there, but actually sucking eagerly on his driver's hot studly filthy asshole. Rico was wanking his cock with his other hand, making loud wet squishy noises in Matt's ears as he hovered his hole over his face. Rico's asshole was clenching and un-clenching and pulsing in Matt's mouth. With his hands bound behind him all Matt could do was as he was told. He felt so degraded yet at the same time he knew that after this he could never resist anything Rico would want from him.

As Matt went on eating Rico's hole Rico told his employer how he would fuck him again someday soon, fuck the shit out of him for hours, non-fucking-stop, he told Matt how he would fuck him until his guts were cramping. He went on about how he would fuck him in the ass until he made Matt piss himself.

"And then I'll just go on and on fucking you pussy Man/Boy," Rico swore. "My hard dick will keep on fucking you, I will keep plunging into you, you'll churn in your guts, I'll totally conquer your executive ass, and I'll make you take it again and again. Then I'll pull my cock out and make you lick it clean. Fucking sheer socked executive, you'll be so fucking overwhelmed by my male sexual power that you'll worship my cock and balls while covered with your own ass juices. You will love it, and you'll love me..."

Matt realized that at that point Rico would own him completely in the sexual arena...

Now, with his hands tied behind him Matt watched as Rico jacked him off. Matt's cum splattered in his stunned face, never before had he cum like that, NEVER so hard and never before bound up with his sheer socks. Rico pissed again on Matt as he shot his load, and then wanked himself off yet again, aiming for his boss's sheer socked feet. He told Matt that he was to wear the same socks and garters again tomorrow to the business meeting he had to attend. Matt nodded and breathlessly said, "Yes Sir."

Later, Rico took the bed and made Matt sleep on the floor, the executive still in his sheer socks and garters. To further humiliate Matt Rico wedged a huge butt-plug in the handsome executive's asshole. Matt felt the heavy weight of it and his semen churned around in his guts. A few times during the night Rico got up to take a leak, right on Matt.

Matt awoke the next morning seeing Rico's beautiful male body standing over him. The driver was holding his cock tight and he let loose with a jet stream of full bladder hot stinking male urine...once again all over poor Matt. He then ordered Matt to piss on himself and he did so, aiming at his own face to get the full taste of his acrid piss...

Somehow Matt made it to his meeting in his piss and cum stained sheer black nylon socks and garters. He was careful though not to cross his leg for fear that one of the men at the meeting would spot the cum on his ankles. When the meeting was concluded and it was the end of the day Rico picked Matt up in his car and brought him back to the hotel. When the door of the hotel room was locked Matt would find out again what the driver's real plans for him were and for more of his fine clothes…

Gassing John Nappi

"Oh naw, no, no, not again yuh blasted mug," I pleaded, begged and beseeched the guy in utter silence as he started the flow of the knockout gas again into one of the thin tubes attached to the over-sized gas mask he (they?) had on me. "Fucker, wh-why are you all doin' this to me???"

My words were silent thoughts actually, only because of the strange plastic round device that was wedged under my lips and against my gums and teeth, forcefully holding my mouth wide open. It was some sort of dentist's device, which is really the only way I can describe the damned thing for you.

On the sides of the strange table (or whatever the fuck it was that I was stretched out on and strapped up to) I was just able to see two or three other guys standing there, laughing meanly. As the gas filled the gas mask I heard their laughter as if from very far away, sort of like in an echo chamber of sorts.

"Awwwwwhhhhrrrrr..." was all I could say as the gas mask filled with the white colored smoke, obscuring what little vision I had of what was just outside the gas mask.

I felt sleepy but tried my best to fight it. Gawds man, how many times did this make that they had pumped the gas mask on me filled with smoke and knocked me out? It seemed that they were having the time of their lives gassing me over and over again. As I felt sleep claiming me one of the guys undid the flap covering on my crotch of the tight leather pants that had my legs encased in. My manhood popped out long, hard and beefy. Just as I fell back into the arms of unconsciousness I felt myself being stroked and made to shoot yet another load for my unseen, unknown captors.

""I-I'm no faggot," I screamed silently and fell asleep. "Awwwwhhhhhhhhhh!"

When I came to I had no idea of how much time had transpired. I only knew that the gas mask was again filling with smoke, pink colored smoke this time. I had come to know this pink gas an aphrodisiac of sorts. It smelled sweet. That's the only way to describe it. Every time I was given the pink gas I felt more than horned up bud. My manhood would start to tingle and my big furry nuts churned like crazy. And shit, every time I was given the pink gas I was jacked off like crazy. Looking up through the smoke and through the big plastic eyeholes of the mask I saw what looked like shadows looming over me. What really amazed me throughout this stranger than strange ordeal was that the gas they pumped into the mask over my head didn't burn my eyes at all.

"Wh-who are you guys?" I silently asked the men looming over and around me.

I heard the sounds of glasses being put down, I heard the sounds of conversation as if in a distance and I heard some of the men gathered around me laughing as I helplessly inhaled the pink gas.

"Awwwwwrrrrhhhhh…" I gurgled in the gas masked prison they had me in.

Besides the gas mask imprisoning my head I was stretched out on a short table that I didn't quite fit on. My legs, encased in a tight fitting pair of leather pants dangled off the end of the table, my feet were bare. I heard, or thought I heard a male voice saying something about keeping my smelly white sweat socks as a souvenir. Jeez, what kind of pervert steals a construction worker's stinking socks to have as a souvenir? *And a souvenir of what?* Just what the fuck was going on here anyway? And I ask you bud, how does a guy explain to his girlfriend that his socks are gone when he gets home? *Was I even going to get home?* Fuck, I'm not ashamed to admit that I was scared shitless man. My upper body, clad in a tight fitting, black leather tee shirt was lain atop the table, strapped down tight, my wrists tied off to the sides of the table and looped to the legs under the table. The table was set at a sort of diagonal position, so I was halfway raised and looking upwards.

What a fucked up sight I was….

And where was I??? That was another million-dollar question. Looking around was virtually impossible. Besides the gas mask with the tubes attached to it on my head obscuring my vision it seemed that my head was immobilized as well. No doubt they had straps over my forehead keeping my head in place, not wanting me to look around at all…

I again heard the sounds of mean laughter and then just barely saw one of the guys out there picking up one of the tubes attached to the gas mask. He puffed at his thick and stinky cigar and then fed me the smoke through the tube. The pink aphrodisiac smoke and the cigar smoke assaulted me as well.

"Awwwhhhrrrrr…" I complained madly, clenching my hands into big meaty fists at my sides.

Then, the flaps on the leather shirt over my nipples were pulled open and I saw two male figures bend over me.

"Looks like its nursing time again huh guys?" I asked them silently.

Then, they were heartily and with real and utter gusto slurping and sucking at my fat pink fleshy nipples. I felt the flap on my crotch being undone as well and I was again being stroked. Fuck, was, was someone licking my bare feet? Oh fuck, someone was sucking one of my big toes, FUCK! FUCKING FUCKERS, they were feasting on me at all ends. GAWD, my tits are real sensitive for a guy's tits! I shot a load, another one, how many I had shot at that point I had no fucking clue bud… Then, I was again given the gas that would carry me back to dreamland… I dreamt, or recalled of how it had all began…

My name is John, John Nappi to be exact. I'm thirty-three years old with salt and pepper colored wavy hair and a thick matching mustache. My eyes are piercing blue and my job as a construction worker keeps me really fit and muscular. One hundred and ninety pounds of sheer hairy muscle that's me dude. I've worked for "Greens and Sons" construction for the last six and a half years now and I've lived with my girlfriend Linda for three of those six and a half years. I'm telling you all this because I want to begin by showing you just how average and how fucking ordinary I am, fuck, nothing special about me that warranted the situation I found myself in that strange night a month or so ago…

It was mid July and the heat was at a fever pitch. I had just put in an eight and a half-hour day in the searing hot sun working outdoors on a construction project. Needless to say I was totally ready to head home, take a nice cool refreshing shower with Linda. (Fuck, but that girl loves when I come home smelling all sweaty and ripe from a long day of slinging two by fours, swinging hammers and lugging cinder blocks.) After that we would have a good dinner and then settle in front of the TV set for a couple of hours. Riding toward home on the train clad in my worn blue jeans, my clonky mustard colored scuffed up work boots and a black tank top with an old button down cotton shirt thrown over it I got the sudden urge for a nice cold beer. The air conditioning vent I was standing under on the train pretty much masked and covered up the sweaty and musty odor I was giving off from my long workday. Yeah, a couple of tall cold beers before heading home would really hit the spot I thought. Linda wouldn't mind after all. So, instead of getting off the train at my usual stop I rode it one more stop to the local watering hole in my neighborhood.

The smell of cigar smoke, cigarettes, stale liquor and beer greeted me as I walked into the dimly lit bar. There were a few guys seated at the front bar and a few seated at the tables off the sides of the bar. I saw four guys in the back of the place engaged in a game of pool. The guys were all dressed either in suits, coming from their office jobs or in construction attire like me. A few of the guys were in shorts and tee shirts, no doubt just neighborhood guys enjoying the free air conditioning.

"What'll it be buddy?" the burly looking bartender asked me as I found a vacant stool at the bar and sat down on it.

"A tall cold Budweiser on tap if you've got it bud," I replied, reaching for my wallet.

"Coming right up," the bartender said and drew the beer from the tap a few inches from where I was sitting. "Hot out there today huh?"

"Sure as shit man," I replied as he set the tall mug of beer in front of me. "I was out there sweating it for more than eight hours today."

"Oh shit, that's awful buddy," the bartender said, taking the ten-dollar bill I handed him and giving me back six dollars.

I left two dollars on the bar.

"Next one is on the house buddy," the bartender said.

"Really?" I asked him. "I didn't see a sign saying that you had a happy hour here."

"We don't," the bartender said. "It's a special for guys like you who were out in this brutal heat all fucking day. Drink up."

"Thanks man, that's really generous of you I got to say," I said with a smile and chugged down a hearty gulp of my beer. "Ahhhh, now that really hits the spot bud."

"Enjoy," the bartender said and moved on to his next patron at the bar.

As I took another good long chug of my beer I suddenly felt a hand on the back of my neck and squeezing.

"Hey there Steve, how's it going?" the guy in the navy blue pinstriped suit asked me as he affectionately squeezed the back of my neck.

"Uh, my name's not Steve, I said, looking up at the blond handsome office guy.

"Oh shit, I'm sorry man," he babbled, still squeezing the back of my neck. "From behind you look just like my good buddy Steve. I'm supposed to be meeting him here in a few minutes and I thought he was early."

"Well, that's nice to hear," I said with a mean looking grin on my face. "But now that you see that I'm not your *buddy* could you please get your hand off my neck?"

"Oh, sure, sure thing man, wow, you even have a big neck like he does," the guy said and squeezed the back of my neck some more.

"I said get your hand off me man," I said, not smiling now.

"Oh yeah, sure," he said, looking a little nervous.

Before he let go though he pressed his thumb hard against the center of the back of my neck and I felt a slight pinch.

"H-hey, wh-what the hell was that?" I asked him, placing my own hand back there now.

"Sorry to have bothered you guy," the suit guy said and walked off in search of his *buddy.*

"Something wrong buddy?" the bartender asked, coming over to me, noticing how I was rubbing the back of my neck, a quizzical expression etched on my face.

"I-I don't know man, th-that faggot came over to me and started feeling me up," I said angrily. "He thought I was his goddamned buddy. I told him to get his hand off my neck and before he did I felt a pinch back there."

"Heh, maybe he thought you were just too fucking handsome for your own good," the bartender chuckled and gave my face a friendly pat. "You about ready for your second beer?"

With my head slightly spinning I looked at my half empty glass.

"Al-almost," I replied. "Listen, do me a favor, check the back of my neck and let me know if you see anything back there. I'm a little afraid of what that faggot just did."

"Sure thing buddy, turn around and I'll take a look," the bartender said.

I turned facing backward on my stool and felt the bartender's fingertips gliding and sliding over the back of my big neck.

"See anything?" I asked him, looking around the bar for the blond suit guy who had pinched me.

"No, nothing back here but a big sweaty neck," the bartender chuckled and then I again felt a pinch back there, this time delivered courtesy of the bartender.

I quickly pulled away, my head spun some more and I turned back on my stool, facing the bartender.

"Wh-whass goin' on here man?" I asked the bartender, suddenly not able to form my words properly.

"I don't understand buddy," the bartender said. "Nothing is going on. Let me get you that free beer."

"Y-you pinssshed the back of m-my neck," I slurred. "J-jus like that blond faggot did. Wh-what are you guys up to here?"

"Sir, I assure you that there is nothing untoward going on here," the bartender said to me with a smile on his face.

Suddenly my vision blurred just as he held my second beer to my lips for me.

"S-say now, I-I can drink my own damned beer," I said stupidly as I was forced to guzzle a good long sip of the brew.

Then, from behind me I heard the familiar voice of the blond suited faggot.

"What'll it be buddy?" I heard the bartender ask him as I sat there with my mouth hanging open and my head spinning.

"I'll have what the construction worker here is having," the blond faggot said. "He looks like whatever he's drinking has him pretty relaxed."

"I-*I relaxed is right dude…* "I slurred, saliva dripping from my mouth and landing on the bar.

"Coming right up," the bartender said to the faggot.

I looked up at the faggot and saw that he was smiling fiendishly at me.

"Wow, you really do look a lot like my buddy," he said and before I could pull away he again had his hand on the back of my neck.

I felt a third pinch and that was when everything went black…for the first time…

As the gas that made me sleep evaporated from the gas mask I again smelled the pink gas being pumped in there.

"Wow, even in his sleep he's hard as a rock," I heard a male voice say and again I was being stroked.

The dream/recall went on. Somehow I remembered more…

After being given the third pinch I slumped forward on the bar, totally unconscious, yet still somehow hearing what was going on around me…

"Hey man, glad you're finally here," I heard the blond suit guy saying to someone. "Take a look at this guy; he sure as hell looks a lot like you."

I felt the back of my hair grabbed and then my head was pulled up. My eyes were half closed and saliva dripped very disgustedly from my gaping mouth.

"Ahhhhwwww, wh-whass happenin'? I gurgled.

"Yeah, he does look a little like me that's for sure," I heard another voice saying. "But this time it's this poor saps turn on the table. He looks enough like me for them to even think it's me. Let's bring him there."

I felt myself being turned on the stool and then two guys lifting me by my arms and legs.

"Here, let me get those boots and socks off him for you," I heard the bartender saying. "We'll give him back his boots when it's all over but I plan to keep his smelly construction worker socks."

"Fuck man, sleazy as ever you are," the guy who I looked like said as he and his suit buddy held my big feet aloft over the bar for the bartender to get to.

Right in sight of everyone in the bar he unlaced my boots and slowly pulled them from my feet, dropping them to the floor behind the bar.

"Whew, I was right, his socks stink like crazy," the bartender said. "What a souvenir these will make."

With that he pulled my socks off my feet, gripping them at the worst part, the moist toes. He sniffed them once, balled them up and quickly packed them in a plastic zip lock bag.

"M-my socks," I mumbled as the two guys carted me now barefooted away from the bar.

I found myself seated on a table, one guy was holding me up and balancing me as other hands worked at getting me stripped. My cotton button down shirt was taken off me and then my tank top was unceremoniously pulled off me over my head, my arms raised above me. I thought I noticed some guys sniffing at my bushy armpits.

"F-faggots?" I asked stupidly as my jeans were shucked off me followed by my raunchy piss and sweat stained white under shorts.

I felt another pinch on the back of my neck and then I was hoisted again.

When I came around again I found that I had been dressed in a pair of very tight fitting black leather pants. They had a button flap right over my crotch area. I was also wearing an extremely tight fitting black leather tee shirt with button flaps on it right over the nipple areas.

"Wh-what the, what the fuck is all this?" I asked stupidly and then the orthodontic device was slid into my mouth and positioned under my gums and against my teeth.

"Awwwrrhrhhhhh," was all I would be saying from that moment on, although my thoughts would be legible but of course unheard by the men holding me captive.

As I lolled on the short table the gas mask was then slid over my head. All that I was able to see was what was out of the immediate area of the plastic eyepieces on the gas mask. It felt like it was pretty heavy so when they laid me down and stretched me out atop the short table it alleviated the pressure somewhat. My legs and bare feet dangled off the end of the table and at the other end so did my head. I lolled my head around trying to see what the fuck was going on and where the fuck I was. But to my dismay and terror my captors got busy strapping me down to the table, good and fucking tight I might add. While they were doing that other guys inserted the tubes into the small holes affixed in the gas mask they had put on me...

Looking through the plastic eyepieces I saw the familiar face of the blond suit faggot who had felt up the back of my neck, although he was no longer so spiffily dressed in a suit now. Rather he was wearing what appeared to be some sort of leather harness over his muscular smooth chest.

"Wh-what the fuck is going on here?" I asked him with my terror filled eyes as he and another guy got the gas mask tightly onto me and inserted the various tubes into it.

"Looks like he's awake again," I heard a faraway voice saying.

"Not for long though," another voice said laughingly.

With that the gas mask began filling with white smoke. I bucked crazily on the table thinking I was going to be gassed to death. As sleep claimed me with the first gassing I felt my cock being brought out of the opening in the leather pants they had on me and then someone was stroking me…

When I opened my eyes I was being given the pink colored gas, the one that when I inhaled it seemed to make me overly horny.

"Arrrrhhhrrrrrwwwwww!" I was crowing as I felt myself shooting a load, someone down there sucking at my dick.

I tried to raise my head but they had somehow immobilized me there. Obviously they had moved me further down the table so that my head was lying on it and my legs now totally dangled off it at the other end.

"Ahhhhrrrrrrrr!" I grunted loudly in the gas mask, the feeling immense as whoever was sucking me was crazily scoffing down my construction worker juices with real gusto.

Where was I? Was I still in the neighborhood bar? What kind of room was this where they did these things?

After spewing my load I felt my cock slipping from the guy's mouth. Trying to look downward to my crotch I simply saw a shadowy figure stand up. Suddenly, two mouths engulfed my exposed nipples. I grunted at the unforeseen feeling of having my man tits worked so soon after shooting my load. Gawd, but I don't like my girlfriend touching my man tits after I shoot a load, being that they're so fucking sensitive, and now I had these faggots feasting on them. I wanted to shout at them to get off my fucking man tits but once again I was given the knockout gas. I had the strangest sensation of someone sucking one of my big toes and my furry balls being licked by what felt like a real big tongue. The gas filled the mask on me and I inhaled it and fell back into the arms of sleep…

When I came to again was when I found that the table I was on had been hoisted up to about sixty degrees, putting me in a sort of diagonal position. Facing somewhat forward now I was able to see shadowy figures walking around the smoke filled dimly lit room I was (being held prisoner) in. Looking around only with my eyes, still not able to move my head I saw a guy standing at the end of the table. He had one of the tubes attached to my gas mask in his hand and the other end of it attached to a box, I think. I could tell that the guy was laughing, looking at me, looking at my exposed cock, balls and man tits.

"Wh-what is all this about?" I asked him silently.

Laughing meanly, his teeth showing real white he flicked a switch on the box and my gas mask was filling with the pink smoke. The guy disappeared from my view and then again I felt the sensation of my cock being sucked…

"Jeez, a guy is sucking my big meat," I said to myself. "Wh-who the fuck has kidnapped me and why???"

As the pink gas filled the gas mask and the guy sucked my cock two other guys found their way over to me and began twisting and kneading my nipples like crazy.

"Awwwrrrhhhhhh!" I crowed helplessly, as the guy sucking me felt more like he was suctioning me.

It went on this way for what felt like an eternity, being made to shoot my load, having my tits, my toes and other parts of me played with and being gassed over and over again. Gassed, to be made to feel horny, gassed to be put to a semi sleep and made to inhale stinking cigar smoke…

"Ohhhhhhhrrrrr," I moaned miserably as I came to a while later, slumped at the bar.

"Hey bud, you okay?" I heard a familiar voice asking me.

I opened my eyes and sat straight up at the bar, facing the bartender.

"St-stay away from me man," I seethed at him. "Don't you or any of those fuckers come near me."

I was staring at him with a look of murder in my steely blue eyes, pointing a shaking finger at him.

"Hey buddy, what's the matter with you?" he asked me. "You fell asleep at my bar and you're pissed with me?"

"F-fell asleep?" I asked him. "Y-you mean you didn't drug me? You didn't dress me up in leather and put a gas mask on me and gas me over and over and milk and suck my cock?"

He looked at me like I was some kind of lunatic.

"Look bud, I don't know what the fuck you're talking about, but I think I can honestly say that two beers is your limit," the bartender said to me, looking at me and looking toward the door to the bar. "I think you'd best be on your way."

I stood up on my booted feet and saw that I was wearing my own clothes. I looked around and saw that the blond guy in the suit was sitting with a rugged guy who looked somewhat like me. He had been right. I did look like his buddy.

"I-I'm on my way," I said to the bartender. "I-I'm really sorry. It was a long day and I think I just had a really bad and fucked up dream."

"I would think so," the bartender said, watching as I made my way to the door.

Outside the warm early evening air caressed me. I took a deep breath and headed for home…

When I walked in the door Linda came rushing to meet me. She greeted me with a kiss and a long hug.

"You're late getting home babe," she said to me as I held her close to me, breathing in the fresh scent of her blond soft hair.

"I stopped off to have a beer at the neighborhood bar," I said into her ear, kissing her earlobe.

"It took you that long to have a beer?" she asked me.

With that I pulled away from her and looked at her questioningly.

"Wh-why? What time is it?" I asked her, terrified of looking at my watch.

"It's after eight o'clock John," she said. "Are you sure you're okay?"

"I-I'm not sure honey," I said to her, heading for the stairs that led to the upstairs bedroom and bathroom. "Uh, let me go and shower and get changed."

"Okay, but dinner is cold," she said. "I'll have to heat it up."

"Yeah, yeah, you do that honey, I-uh, I have to check on something," I said, glancing down at my boots as I raced up the stairs.

Oh God, Oh God, I thought, if my socks were gone I knew that it would have all been real. But if my socks were still on my feet I would know that I had been dreaming all of it...

With my hands and fingers trembling I hastily unlaced my work boots...

When my boots were unlaced I shucked them off my feet and looked down...

Jose the Model

"Do you really theenk that thees ees a good idea?" the beyond handsome Spanish model asked me in his thick accent, sounding totally bewildered as I held the slack of the rope that was tied tightly around his upper body in my hand, pulling the slack, tying him tighter still.

"It's a *great* idea, trust me Jose," I said to the naïve guy as he stood there clad in just the white and lime green striped briefs he had been hired to model that day. "Bondage, things like S&M are all out of the closet and in our faces these days. What better way to sell those briefs you've got on? Believe me, the pictures that I'll take of you like this will sell those briefs faster than anyone will ever imagine."

"S&M?" Jose asked me, looking at me sideways as I tied him tighter still, winding more rope around and around his upper body. "What ees thees S&M?"

"It's an abbreviation for the words sadism and masochism," I explained, truly enjoying my job as a photographer on that day. "It's what a lot of people nowadays are into in the bedroom area of their lives. Look at it as a form of domination and submission if you will."

"And you really theenk that thees S&M as you call it weel help to sell the breefs I wear?" he asked me, seeming to look very nervous and embarrassed at the same time as I wallowed in binding him up tighter and tighter.

"Jose, I assure you, that because of you the briefs will sell like hotcakes, trust me on this while I truss you okay?" I replied sounding somewhat sinister.

I still couldn't believe that the guy had allowed me to get him tied up. Actually, once I'd started winding the rope around him there wasn't much he could do to stop me.

"I steel do not understand," the exotically handsome, six foot three inch tall Spanish model said in his thick Spanish accent, turning his head facing forward, a look of utter confusion on his handsome chiseled featured face. "All I know right now is that you are tying me up real tight. I am feeling very strange as you would say I theenk."

"Just relax and go with it Jose," I said reassuringly. "Once I have you tied the way I want you I'll start taking pictures. I'll give you instructions on how to struggle as you pose. Being the good model that you are I'm sure you'll take my directions very well. We'll be done real quickly. Then you won't have to feel so strange anymore, okay?"

"Eef you say so Mr. Porter," Jose said, sounding resigned to what I was doing to him.

"Okay, come on; help me out here a little okay Jose?" I asked him, pulling on the slack of the rope, pinning his long arms to his upper body at his sides. "Turn yourself around slowly so the rope winds nice and evenly around you."

He did as I said and as he turned I pulled the rope tighter around him, getting some good grunts and groans out of him.

"Good guy Jose," I said to him with a smile as we faced each other for a moment. "This spread of pictures of you is going to be so hot, so great that those briefs are going to fly off the shelves in the stores after people see the shots I'm going to take of you."

"Do you really theenk so Mr. Porter?" Jose asked, sounding more and totally unsure of the situation he was now in. "I mean all of thees just so that we can sell some breefs?"

"I know so man, I truly know so," I replied, taking in the exquisite sight of his melon shaped ass cheeks as they filled the briefs he was in beautifully. "When women see the ads for these briefs they're going to want to tie their boyfriends up, just like I'm doing to you right now. When men see the ads for them they'll want their wives and girlfriends to tie them up. Perhaps we'll say in the ad that our briefs will have you so in love that you'll be tied up in knots."

I had all to do to keep from stealing a squeeze or a few of his round bubble butt cheeks.

"Never modeled like thees before when I was een my country," the model said as I tied him and tied him.

"Where are you from Jose?" I asked him, trying to make some general conversation, trying to get his mind off the fact that he was being tied up tighter and tighter. (*Right…*)

"I am from Santo Domingo," the fair skinned exotically handsome guy said. "I came here a leetle less than a year ago now."

"Wow, a little less than a year and you speak English so well," I said.

"Oh, you are only humoring me as you Americans say Meester Porter," he said with a grin, facing me again, his beautiful dark eyes beguiling me. "I steel have so much English to learn. But I am glad that modeling helps pay thee bills, as you Americans say."

Holding what was left of the slack of the rope I pulled the guy a few steps forward, his big fat pink nipples on his smooth chest looking at me temptingly. God almighty, they were like two eraser nubs on his lanky well-defined chest.

"How old are you Jose?" I asked him, turning him around, facing away from me so I could get the rope knotted tight.

"Twenty-seex," he responded. "My birthday was last month."

"Happy birthday," I said to him, pulling the rope tighter behind him. "And many more."

The lanky, very tall (as I said) exotically handsome Spanish model was standing on a rubber mat in my photography studio where I had positioned him for the photo shoot. He was clad in just a pair of the name brand briefs he was to model for me, white and lime green striped cotton tighties. On the phone he had told me he wore a size "large" when it came to underpants. When he arrived for the shoot I profusely apologized for only having the size "medium" for him to pose in. Standing there in his jeans, pull over shirt and Western boots and holding the briefs in his hand he looked at me, looking unsure. His silky black hair and piercing dark eyes combined sent shivers through me. I did my best to remain calm as I plotted how to have some real kinky fun with this very obviously naïve guy. I explained that the company who made the briefs must have made the mistake in sending me the incorrect size. Then, he simply nodded, said they would do and asked where he should get changed. I pointed to the bathroom and told him to meet me on the rubber mat that was set up in the center of my studio. I noticed as he walked toward the bathroom that he was extremely lanky and bowlegged. His thighs practically rubbed together as he walked his lower leg's spread sort of strangely wide. I figured that the agency that represented him had taken him on for the purposes of underwear and bathing suit modeling. The way his legs spread out at the bottom and the way they nearly rubbed together at the thighs gave him a good bikini look. He stepped into the bathroom closing the door behind him. I heard the sounds of his boots hitting the floor as he took them off. As he got changed in the bathroom I quickly looked over the file folder the agency had sent on him. It contained numerous head shots of him, pictures of him in business attire, pictures of him in casual and formal attire (he really did justice to a tuxedo let me tell you) and a few pictures of him in a red Speedo bikini on a beach in Santo Domingo. The agency had sent me the file on Jose to look over based on the product he was to model. When I saw the pictures of him in the bikini on the beach I knew he was the one for the upcoming underwear ads. I was right in my assumption where his being bowlegged was concerned and how well he would fill out a pair of sexy underpants. Looking at the head shots of his beguilingly handsome face smiling at me my mind had started churning with some mean and wicked ideas. I knew that if I attempted what I had in mind I could get into more than a shit load of trouble. Still looking at the pictures of him and grinning I also thought that if I attempted what I had in mind it could very well go the other way, meaning that the modeling guy would love the scene. The girl at the agency who sent me his file told me that Jose spoke broken English, had been in the country less than a year but that he was a great and friendly guy to deal with. The file folder also contained letters of praise and recommendation from photographers in his country that he had posed for over the last few years. When Jose arrived at my studio I offered him a cold drink, citing that I had iced tea, soda, even beer if he wanted it. He said that he was fine and simply wanted to get to work. He was an all work type of guy. I liked that in him instantly. I went over the shoot with him, reminding him that he would be posing in just the name brand briefs that the company had hired me to photograph him in. He said that was no problem, until of course I showed him the one size small underpants they'd sent me. Now granted I had never attempted with other guys who had modeled for me what I was about to attempt with Jose. It was something in his looks that seemed to spur me on. Jose emerged from my bathroom a few minutes later wearing the briefs I had given him to put on and his knee length navy blue nylon dress socks. He took a few steps toward me and said he was ready. The bulge in his crotch evidenced that the guy was truly gifted in that area. No wonder he had seemed nervous about posing in a size smaller than what he had told me he was in briefs. His dick made a real impression in the thin cotton material. I had to hold back a gasp at the sight of him in just those briefs and his socks. His feet were easily size ten and a half, if not a little bigger. The way those feet were outlined in his thin socks had me salivating just as much as the bulge he was sporting in the briefs. Taking him by his upper arm I walked him to the spot on the mat in front of my cameras where I intended to photograph him.

"Have you ever done any underwear ads before?" I asked him, loving the way his filled out crotch area moved in the tighties.

"No, only bikini ads," he said, telling me what I already knew.

"Okay Jose, let me explain a few things to you then about modeling underwear here in America," I said, stepping behind him and grasping him now by both his upper arms, positioning and balancing him in front of my cameras. "People in America like kinky underwear ads, not ordinary ads. Do you understand?"

"Keenky? What means thees keenky?" Jose asked, sounding totally confused as I let go of his arms and stepped in front of him, taking in the sight of his lanky well-toned smooth torso area.

"Kinky, it means a little daring, *very sexy,*" I replied, giving his chest a friendly swat with the back of my hand.

"Oh, I see," he laughed a little nervously. "But how are you going to make me look sexy as you Americans say? I am plain vanilla I would theenk."

Jeez, the guy had no clue just how much he had going for him in the area of his looks that was for sure.

"Well, as far as I'm concerned you look sexy already," I said to him, glancing down at the briefs as they hugged his crotch and butt cheeks. "Now we just need to get you looking...kinky, as I said."

"And how weel you do that Mr. Porter?" he asked me, not having once moved from the position I had posed him in.

He was a perfect and professional model that was for sure.

"Well, there are numerous ways we can achieve that Jose," I said, rubbing my chin, as if I were deep in thought.

"Numerous ways?" he asked me. "What is one way?"

"Well, do you know what bondage is Jose?" I asked him, pretending to adjust the front section of his briefs by pulling on the elastic waistband of them.

"Bowndage?" he asked me in his broken English.

"No, bondage," I said, stepping a few feet away from him and opening the drawer of a nearby desk, taking out and holding out a pile of white cotton rope. "Bondage, meaning to tie someone up."

"Tie someone up?" he asked nervously. "You mean mee Mr. Porter?"

"Just for the pictures Jose," I explained, approaching him with the rope. "It'll drive people crazy when they see the ads. It'll be very, as I said, kinky. What do you think?"

"I don't know Meester Porter," the handsome model said, sounding totally unsure.

I stepped next to him, said, "Let's give it a try" and before he could protest I pulled a good length of the rope around his upper body, pressing his arms against his sides. His hands were splayed out at his sides his fingers all spread wide. He stood there looking real sexy in a bowlegged position. A look of total astonishment filled his face as I began winding the rope around him.

"The rope is made of pure cotton Jose," I said to him. "It won't leave marks and it won't burn your skin. You okay so far?"

"Yes, I suppose so," he said, looking down at his chest as I wound the rope just above and then under his nipples, making a nice showcase of them.

"See? I told you it would be great to photograph you this way in those briefs," I said to the guy.

He looked up at the ceiling, took a deep breath and looked back down.

"Eet feels strange," he said, trying to grin in the strange situation I'd just thrust him into.

A few moments later I had his upper body tied, his nipples jutting out of the ropes, as I said I'd made a nice showcase of them.

"I have to get these socks off you Jose," I said, before getting to work winding more rope around his stomach area. "Is that okay? The magazine wants you in just your briefs. If I photograph you in these long socks it won't be what they're looking for. Your long socks are kissing your knees."

"Yes, go ahead, you can take my socks off me," Jose said as I squatted down in front of him, his crotch right in my face. "Heh, my socks are keesing my knees. Now that sounds sexy as you Americans say, or maybe eeven keenky."

Looking down he watched and held himself balanced as I pushed his long blue nylon socks down around his ankles and then off his big feet. I managed to inhale a good nose-full of his crotch scent while I was down there getting his socks off him. Heaven, pure, fucking heaven to say the least. I stood up with the guy's long socks in my hand and without a word placed them in one of the back pockets of my jeans, making them stick halfway out. Jose looked a little confused as to why I'd just put his socks in my jeans pocket but then I started winding more rope around him, pinning his lower arms to his body now...

After I'd wished the guy a belated happy birthday I was done tying him and it was time to start taking pictures. *And,* what I had hoped for was starting to happen...

I stepped over to the first camera that I planned to use and looked for Jose through the viewfinder.

"Okay Jose, lets get this show on the road," I said to him, looking at his blank faced expression through the view-finder. "When I tell you to start struggling I want you to give me a good show, got it?"

I snapped a few test-shots of him looking real glum and nervous in the tight bondage.

"Struggle, how do you mean thees struggle?" he asked me, squirming in the bondage.

"Pretend you're trying to get untied, I explained to him, moving the camera up and down, and scanning his lanky body and his bow legs.

"Oh yes, now I understand," he said and half-smiled.

He clenched his teeth and started struggling against the ropes.

"Good Jose, very good," I said enthusiastically and snapped picture after picture of him.

"Like you say here een America, you do not have to tell me twice," Jose said. "I want to be untied soon Mr. Porter."

"Just do as I'm instructing you and you'll be untied real soon and…uh-oh," I said and stopped taking pictures.

I looked at Jose with disappointment showing on my face.

"Ees there a problem Mr. Porter?" he asked me.

"Well, as you can see you've chubbed up in your briefs Jose," I said, trying to sound as irritated over this fact as possible.

"Chubbed up in my briefs?" he asked, repeating what I'd just said to him. "What does this mean, chubbed up in my briefs?"

"It means you've got a hard-on, an erection," I said, explaining and pointing at his crotch as I slowly approached him. "People who see the ads aren't going to want to see that. They're supposed to get turned on, not you."

"I-I deedn't mean for that to happen," he said, sounding apologetic as I stood before him. "Sometimes eet just has a mind of eets own, as you would say I theenk."

"Well, it looks like I'm going to have to help you out with this problem Jose," I said and placed a hand over the bulge in his briefs.

He was harder than a rock in those tighties and throbbing like crazy. Moving my hand over his crotch I felt his big bulging balls churning in the briefs. Fuck me but I got the feeling that the guy was chock filled with his love juices. I got the feeling that the photo shoot was going to go a little longer than I had expected.

"Wh-what are you doing Meester Porter?" Jose asked me, sounding a tad more than nervous now as I began slowly stroking him in the briefs.

"Just want to help you lose the chub Jose," I said and a thick pearl of pre cum seeped through the thin material of his briefs.

Looking down Jose saw more and more droplets of his good stuff forming on the briefs.

"B-but it will soil the briefs," he said, sounding more confused now. "Ohhhhhh Meester Porter…"

"Not a problem Jose," I said reassuringly. "The company that makes the briefs sent over plenty of pairs as back-ups."

"An-and all in size medium?" he asked me. "Ohhhhhhhh…"

"Yeah, sorry about that Jose, all in size medium," I said with a half-smile on my face.

"B-but Meester Porter, I-I am going to shoot my load in my breefs," he panted, gyrating himself, trying his best to stay in the position I'd posed him in.

"Not a problem Jose," I said and stroked him in the tighties a little faster, my other hand cupping the outline of his juicy and sweaty balls now, squeezing them gently.

"Ohhhhhhhhh, f-feels so strange to have you do thees to me," he said and looked up at the ceiling, his mouth halfway open, his lips quivering. "I-I am getting close as you would say."

"Just let it go Jose, then I'll get the briefs off you and get another pair onto you, then we'll resume the photo shoot," I said to him.

He quickly looked down and looked at me in alarm as I stroked him faster.

"Y-you will take the briefs off me?" he asked. "W-won't you untie me so I can get changed?"

"No time for that," I said and then his eyes crossed.

"Ohhhhhhhhh I-I theenk I am cumming Meester Porter," he grunted.

"Just let it go Jose," I said to him reassuringly, letting him know that it was just fine. "It's all so that the photo shoot will be a success."

"Ohhhhhhh, y-yes, th-th photo shoot," the model said and with his eyes crossed and a look of bewilderment adorning his face he filled the briefs with his thick creamy juices. "Ooooooooo, g-got me creeeming in my breefs, as you would say."

He bent slightly at the knees, splayed his long fingers out on both hands and quivered in a very sexy way from side to side.

"N-never had a photo guy do thees to me before Meester Porter," Jose said as I squeezed the last of his load from him.

He stood there panting, catching his breath as I got a medium-sized plastic zip lock bag from a cabinet. Then, keeping himself balanced he watched totally dumbfounded as I slid the cum sopped briefs off him and deposited them into the zip lock bag.

"Do you always cross your eyes like that when you shoot your load Jose?" I asked him, taking in the sight of his uncut at least nine to ten inch slimy dick as it hung semi hard over two of the juiciest looking Spanish balls I had ever seen.

"I-I don't know Meester Porter," the model replied, looking down at himself, hunching his shoulders and gulping softly. "I nayver watch my eyes when I shoot my load. Oh my, y-you have mee naked here."

"Not to worry Jose," I said quickly.

I dropped the zip lock containing his cum sopped briefs on a table and quickly produced a fresh pair. Squatting in front of him I helped the guy into the new briefs. He looked totally embarrassed and totally humiliated as I got the briefs on him. Once again his manhood made a very nice impression in the thin fabric of the tighties.

"On with the photo shoot?" I asked him, stepping behind him, taking him by the upper arms and positioning him back properly on the mat.

"Yes pleese, back to the photo shoot," the handsome model said agreeably, but sounding dismayed at the same time.

"Good guy," I said and gave him a light swat on the ass.

I got behind the first camera again and again looked for Jose through the viewfinder.

"Okay Jose, just like before I want you to struggle like crazy in the bondage," I instructed him. "Only this time I want you to clench your teeth and arch your back a little. Make it look like you're really angry and want more than anything to be untied."

"Heh, that weel be easy," the model said. "I do want to be untied Meester Porter..."

He did as I had instructed him and I have to say he put on quite a show for me, gnashing his teeth, arching his back, balling his fingers into fists and struggling like a madman to pull free of the tight bondage.

"That's it Jose, you got it down just right, struggle, struggle like your life depended on it," I said as I snapped picture after picture of him.

When I was done with the first camera I moved to the second camera I had set up, this one containing black and white film and special attachments for added effect in the pictures. I noticed Jose glancing at his socks sticking out of the back pocket of my jeans as I moved to my other camera. He licked his lips nervously as I began looking for him through the viewfinder of my second camera.

"Okay Jose, now for these pictures I want you to struggle just as you did a few moments ago," I said to him. "The only difference will be that these pictures will be black and white and some of them will be close ups as well. Understand?"

"I understand," he replied and prepared to put himself into a struggling position.

"Stop Jose, *stop*," I said, sounding irritated all over again.

"Eees there a problem Meester Porter?" he asked me, trying to pretend that he didn't know he'd laid another hard in the new briefs I had on him.

"Well, you obviously don't need for me to tell you that you've chubbed up again in your briefs," I said, slowly approaching him, feigning irritation.

"Y-yes, eet would look that way Meester Porter," the model said, glancing down at his hard on as it pressed against the thin fabric of the briefs, pearls of pre cum oozing through them. "As I said, eet seems to have a mind of eet's own."

"Looks like I'll have to help you along again Jose," I said and this time slid the briefs down in the front, tucking them under his big juicy balls.

His hard on pointed straight up at heaven, his foreskin totally slid back on it. With no hesitation whatsoever I took his slimy cum coated manhood in hand and began slowly stroking the beyond exotically handsome model.

"Ohhhhhhhh, ohhhh no, not again Meester Porter," Jose gasped, looking down in horror at his exposed manhood and the fact that I was sliding him in and out of his foreskin. (Watching his hardness disappear in and out of that sexy foreskin was certainly a sight to see let me tell you.) "C-couldn't you just untie me and let me do thees myself Meester Porter? Ohhhhhhhhhhh…"

"As I told you Jose, we really don't have time for that," I said, stroking him a tad faster, squishing sounds emanating from his manhood in my hand as I worked his foreskin up and down and up and down.

He stood there tottering on his feet, looking real sexy, sweating slightly as I worked his manhood.

"Ohhhhhhhh I-I am so sensitive and sexy down there after I shoot a load Meester Porter," Jose panted. "And you are driving me crazy now, as you Americans would say I theenk."

"I'll say you're sexy Jose," I chuckled. "Like I told you before when people see the ads we're doing here for these underpants they're going to buy them faster than the stores can stock them."

"I-I hope so Meester Porter," Jose began, but then stopped in mid sentence as his second load erupted from him in gushes. "Ohhhhhhhhhhhh I-I am cumming again Meester Porter! Ohhhhhhhh…"

He arched his back and grimaced as his mess splashed and splattered all over his lanky and well-toned torso.

"Ohhhhhhh aynd so soon at that," he gasped in his thick accent as I stroked and squeezed every possible droplet of his precious juices from him.

"Looks like we'll need to get you into another pair of underpants huh Jose?" I asked him, sliding the underpants off him again without having even asked his permission this time.

"I-I suppose so Meester Porter," he said as I used the second pair of underpants to wipe all his mess off his chest, his stomach area and his nipples, teasingly squeezing his nipples a few times each as I ran the underpants over them.

"Ohhhhhhhh…" he reeled as I played squeeze with his man tits.

"You got sensitive nipples eh Jose?" I asked him.

"Y-yes Meester Porter, please don't squeeze them," he said. "Oh my, I am naked again…"

A few minutes later I had the guy clad in a third pair of the underpants that he had been hired to model for me. I had put the second cum soiled pair in the plastic zip lock bag along with the first pair. He stood there positioned and ready as I stood behind him tying a black silk blindfold over his eyes for this part of the photo session.

"M-meester Porter, wh-why are you covering my eyes?" he asked me. "Don't you like my eyes?"

"I think your eyes are great Jose," I said, knotting the silk blindfold in the back of his head. "But lots of people use blindfolds on their sex partners. It's a way of teasing the person who is already tied up, makes them wait and wonder where the next touch is coming from. Also, it enhances the bondage you're in. Understand?"

"I-I am not sure Meester Porter," Jose replied as I made my way back over to my camera. "All I know ees that this is the strangest photo shoot I have ever done."

"I'll agree with you there Jose," I said with a chuckle. "Now, once again, please struggle in the bondage like you're trying to pull free."

"No problem again Meester Porter," Jose said and this time I swear he really did struggle like a crazed madman.

"Excellent Jose, superb," I said and snapped pictures of him like crazy. "Now, arch your lower body forward, show me the name brand stitched into the front of those briefs."

He did as I instructed him and I shot more pictures.

"RRRRRRRRR...want to be untied soon Meester Porter," Jose grunted through clenched teeth as I snapped pictures.

"Of course Jose," I said. "Of course. And once you're untied we'll do some regular underwear shots."

"Y-yes Meester Porter," Jose said, sounding a little nervous.

Through my viewfinder I saw the bulge that Jose was sporting in the newest pair of briefs I had put on him.

I smiled wickedly from ear to ear...

It looked like this particular photo shoot would go on all day...

I was glad I didn't have any other appointments for that day...

I stopped taking pictures, walked over to the blindfolded tied up model and again got his manhood out of his underpants. He gasped loudly as I began stroking his slimy dick...

"M-meester Porter, I hope you have lots of pairs of breefs," Jose said, grinning behind his blindfold.

I stroked him faster...

Horatio

Author's Note: The next little tidbit is actually an essay that when looking at it in retrospect I am thinking it should have been included in my recent book, "Quirks." This essay was inspired by an extremely sexy Spanish guy who works in my office. I changed his name for the purposes of this little tale, but overall I am sure he knows who he is…

The Essay:

It was the nuttiest thing that I had ever heard, but what the hell, it was a way for me to earn twenty five easy dollars, *twenty five dollars man,* and all it would cost me was my damned socks. Of all things man, that guy who works across the office from me, he wanted my socks, *my goddamned smelly and worn socks at that bud,* go figure. I'm laughing as I write this because over the years I've heard the strangest things, but wanting a guy's used socks? No man that was a new one let me tell you, even for me. It was a morning like any other that day when I'd settled down at my desk at work. I work for a bank in Manhattan, I'm a suit and tie guy. The guy who wanted my socks works across the office from where I sit, and I suppose from where I sit and the position my feet are in gave him a great view of my damned socks. Fuck, I'm still laughing as I write this because it was the craziest thing man, I mean, who pays attention to a guy's damned socks after all? I guess it can be said now that my office buddy does, because till this moment in time *he has* those socks of mine. He keeps them in a plastic zip-lock bag bud. My worn and smelly black nylon dress socks man, in a plastic zip-lock bag, in my office buddy's possession. What a thing huh? Anyway, as I said it was a morning like any other that day when I settled down at my desk upon my arrival at work. I had my brown paper bag with my coffee and a bagel in it in one hand and my folded up newspaper under my arm, in my other hand was my attaché case. My office buddy was already at his desk that morning that was the first thing that I found to be strange that day, seeing as I'm usually the first one in every morning.

"Hey good morning Chris," I called over him, putting my attaché case down on my desk and waving over at him.

"Good morning Horatio," he called back as I sat down in my chair, taking my container of coffee from the bag as I did so.

I leaned back in my chair to sip my coffee and saw Chris get to his feet and then slowly the guy made his way over to my desk.

"Got a minute?" he asked me as I took a bight of my bagel.

I nodded "yes" and swallowed and said, "Sure, what's on your mind?"

"Well, I figured I would talk to you about this before everyone else got here," he replied, looking like he was about to turn four different shades of red from embarrassment.

"What is it?" I asked him and took another bight of my bagel, crossing one leg on my knee as he spoke to me, giving him a great view of my OTC black nylon sock, the kind that I wear nearly everyday.

"Well, you see, I have a little bet going on where you're concerned Horatio," Chris said to me.

"A bet? You have a bet going on about me?" I asked him. "With who? Someone I know? What kind of bet man?"

"Well, yeah, it's a bet about you and it's with a buddy of mine," Chris said and by now I was smiling, feeling very flattered somehow that I had become the subject of a bet between two friends. "He doesn't work here so you don't know him."

"Okay, I'm cool with this so far," I said, watching as Chris nervously tugged at his tie. "So, what's the bet all about?"

"Well, it's not just a bet, it's a chance for you to make twenty five dollars," Chris said and I nearly blanched.

"Twenty five dollars?" I asked him, nearly spilling my coffee as I raised the container to my lips.

"Yeah, well, if I win the bet my buddy has to give me fifty dollars," Chris said, and at that moment I saw him stealing glances at my socked calf as it rested on my knee. "If I win I'll share the loot with you, but I won't tell him that of course."

"Of course," I said, grinning now. "So dude, what's the bet? What do I have to do to help you win fifty dollars?"

"Well, it's really going to sound strange when I tell you, which is why I got here so early this morning," Chris said. "I didn't want anyone else hearing this when we talked. I mean, if you say no when I ask you what I have to ask you

I hope that you'll just forget about it and pretend like this conversation never happened."

Now I was intrigued man, fuck, I was beyond intrigued. This was becoming more and more curious with each passing second.

"Uh, look I'm not going to have to do anything sexual right?" I asked Chris, now me tugging nervously at my tie as well. "I mean dude, I'm a married guy you know? And I love my wife and…"

"No, no, nothing like that at all Horatio," Chris said reassuringly.

I mean, I knew that the guy was gay, but honestly, from the bottom of my heart (and my feet?) it didn't bother me at all. My policy on stuff like that is live and let live.

"Okay, well now that we cleared the air on that, tell me what the bet is all about," I said, sounding totally inquisitive now.

"The bet is about your socks," Chris said to me and for a few seconds we just stared at each other, then, we both looked down at my black socked calf as it rested on my knee, and then we looked back up at each other again…

I thought for sure he was joking.

"My socks?" I asked Chris. "The bet is about my socks?"

"Yeah," Chris said and now he did turn red, a nice pinkish red, but he turned red nonetheless.

"What is it about my socks that you bet on dude?" I asked, smiling from ear to ear as I asked the question. "If you bet that they smell real funky at the end of the day then you win bud. If you bet that my wife hates handling them when she has to take them from the hamper to put them in the washing machine then you win again. If you bet that since I'm married I have never bought a pair of socks, seeing as my wife buys them for me all the time then you win hands down. Do I get my twenty five dollars now?"

"No, although those are things that my buddy and I talked about when we made the bet," Chris said.

I laughed loudly at that point in disbelief and said, "You and whoever this buddy or yours is talked about my socks and how they smell?"

This was too much, but as I said at the outset, twenty five dollars is twenty five dollars man…

"Well yeah, but that's only part of the bet Horatio," Chris said.

"What's the other part?" I asked him and took a long sip of my coffee.

I noticed how he waited till I had swallowed my coffee before he told me the clincher, the punch line, the topper if you would…

"I bet my buddy that I could get you to give me a pair of your day old socks at the end of the workday sometime," Chris said to me and to be perfectly honest I nearly jumped out of my socks in shock.

"You bet that you could get me to give you a pair of my socks at the end of the day?" I asked him, wiggling my toes under my socks in my shoes at that point.

I guess all this talk about my damned socks of all things had gotten me involuntarily wiggling my little piggies.

"You mean to say that you want me to give you my worn smelly socks at the end of the day???" I asked my office buddy incredulously.

"Yeah, like I said, if I succeed in this I'll win the bet and you and I get twenty five dollars each," Chris said, sounding very nervous now. "Now granted, twenty five dollars really isn't that much money these days, but shit, a bets a bet you know? And ha, ha, think of all the socks you could buy with twenty five dollars."

I mulled it over a few moments and then asked the obvious question...

"Why me?" I asked and sipped my coffee.

"Well, it's a long story," Chris said.

"Give me the condensed version then," I said, gripping my black socked calf as I spoke, teasing my buddy at the same time.

I had already decided that he could have my damned socks, but fuck; I did need to make him squirm a bit didn't I?

"Well, my buddy who I made the bet with, he has a bit of a foot fetish, and I guess I do, at times," Chris said, sounding more and more nervous.

"A foot fetish?" I asked, becoming more and more intrigued and then remembering the times when I noticed Chris looking across the office at me, glancing down at my feet as I rested them behind my chair as I worked. "At times you have a foot fetish? *At times?*"

"Okay, all the time," Chris said and I smiled real big and let go of my calf, giving the guy back the view of my sock.

Hell, at that moment I even recalled how sometimes when I wore slip-on dress shoes how I would slide them off my feet during the day while sitting at my desk. For me it was relaxing to let my feet breathe a bit out of my shoes, for Chris it was sheer (no pun intended) ecstasy I suppose. I could see where Chris would have chosen me for his bet with his buddy. But a foot fetish, and *my socks???* I had never thought of my socked feet as erotic in any way, but hell, to each his own you know? I mean, when I put my socks on in the morning I don't give it a second thought, but obviously Chris and his buddy did.

"That's great dude, a foot fetish, of all things," I said, taking a bight of my bagel and chewing it slowly.

"Yeah, it's harmless enough," Chris said, squirming more and more now and admittedly I loved making him squirm.

"So what does you and your buddy having foot fetishes have to do with my socks and you wanting them?" I asked him, tugging at my tie, and a sly look in my eyes now.

'Well, recently he and I were talking about our mutual fetish and we were swapping stories about guys we knew who have great looking feet," Chris replied and I started to understand. "You see, my buddy, he works in construction and he wishes he could work around guys who wear dark colored dress socks, guys like you and me Horatio…"

"Okay, cool," I said, sliding my foot off my knee ad placing it back on the floor next to my other foot.

"He said that there's one guy at the jobsite who wears thin black dress socks with his construction boots," Chris went on about his construction buddy.

"Oh man, that's nasty dude, those socks of his must stink to the highest heavens at the end of the day after being encased in a pair of heavy clonky work boots," I said and Chris simply grinned at me.

"Exactly, *dude,*" Chris said, mimicking me and we both laughed, the tension in the air seeming to be released somehow.

"Needless to say my buddy said how he would pay money if he was able to get his hands on that guy's stinky dress socks at the end of the day, after they'd been squished into his work boots, sleazy I know, but kinky still the same," Chris went on. "When he said he would pay money to have the guy's socks was when I mentioned you and how you always tend to wear thin black dress socks with your suits."

"Yeah, that's me dude, thin black dress socks from Monday to Friday and thick white sweat socks on the weekends," I said. "I'm what I guess a lot of people would call a regular type of guy…"

"Yeah, I would think so…" Chris responded.

"Now, let me see if I can figure out the rest of this," I said, holding up a hand.

"Okay, cool," Chris laughed.

"After your foot fetish buddy told you how he would love to have his construction worker's buddy's socks after he'd been wearing them all day you told him about me and how I wear thin black dress socks, practically everyday at that," I said, sounding like the office manager that I am.

"Yeah, that's how it started out," Chris said.

"And I'll bet, I will just bet that your buddy said he would love to have my socks," I said, wagging a finger at Chris in a teasing manner. "After you told him how handsome and debonair I am…"

"Well, no, I said that I would love to have your socks," Chris said and I

126

nearly fell off my chair. "That's how the bet came about…"

"I see," I said, watching as Chris looked down at my feet.

"My buddy told me that he would bet money that I couldn't get you to give me your socks," Chris continued, looking back up at me after peeling his stare off my feet. "So in turn I told him he was on, and we bet fifty dollars where your socks are concerned.

"My goddamned socks," I laughed, holding my hands over my washboard stomach area as I chuckled in my seat.

"So, what do you think?" Chris asked lowering his voice as office personnel started filing in for the workday ahead.

"I'll have to let you know dude," I said, getting to my feet. "I have to go to the computer room and get my reports…see you later…"

Chris looked totally stupefied as I stepped out from behind my desk, gave his shoulder a squeeze and left the office. I think he'd regretted telling me about his little bet…

It was when I'd returned from lunch that I told Chris my decision…

He was sitting at his desk working on some stuff on his pc when I walked over to him. Like early in the mornings most of the staff wasn't there so there was no one to overhear our conversation… Just about everyone in Chris' area takes lunch at the same time.

"Hey there dude, I just got back from lunch," I said with a snide looking grin on my face. "Did a little shopping while I was out…"

Still grinning I held up a small bag from Brooks Brother's men's store which is right near our office…

"What'd you get?" Chris asked, obviously still squirming from the way I'd left him hanging and in suspense over his bet and his special request.

Instead of answering him verbally I reached into the Brooks Brothers bag and held up a new pair of thin OTC black nylon dress socks. Actually, they matched the ones I was wearing that day…

"What'd you buy socks for?" Chris asked me.

"Well, you don't expect me to go home after work with no socks on do you?" I asked him in reply and when he saw the look in my eyes his whole face seemed to light up. "Hey dude, twenty five dollars is twenty five dollars right?"

"Sure thing man,' Chris said, looking totally delighted.

"After everyone goes home we'll do this," I said, putting the new socks back in the bag. "And we'll even work some overtime, that way I can really sweat up my socks for you during the rest of the day…"

With that same devilish looking grin on my face I sauntered back to my desk, swinging the Brooks Brother's bag as I went…

At five forty five in the evening Chris and I were the only two people left in the office…

He stood in front of my desk, watching intently as I unlaced my wingtips. He was holding a plastic zip lock bag in his hands and his hands were shaking. I shucked my shoes off my feet, placed them on the floor and then Chris watched just as intently as I slowly took my black socks off. He opened the zip lock bag, ready to receive the prize he sought; I leaned forward and deposited the prize that Chris coveted for into the plastic baggie. Chris quickly zipped the zip lock shut and slipped it into the inside pocket of his suit jacket.

"Twenty five dollars bud," Chris said and handed me the money. "Enjoy it…"

"And you enjoy the socks," I said, smiling at the dude, my bare feet feeling real strange under my desk.

I mean, let's face it; I have never, for any reason whatsoever been barefoot at work…

"God, there's something so hot about having a guy's used smelly socks in your possession," Chris said. "Thanks Horatio."

"If you say so dude," I laughed and put the twenty five dollars in my wallet.

"And of course this is just between us right?" Chris asked me.

"Scouts honor man," I said, crossing my heart the way we did when we were kids. "I mean, who would believe this anyway?"

"You'd be surprised," Chris responded and patted his suit jacket where my socks now were. "Anyway, I'll see you tomorrow Horatio. Thanks a lot man. I can't wait to show my buddy these socks of yours."

"One question before you go," I called out as Chris headed for the door. "How will your buddy know they're my socks and not a pair of yours that you just put in that zip lock bag?"

"Oh, that's easy, he knows how my socks smell," Chris said and then it was his turn to grin devilishly at me.

He said good night again and left the office...

I sat at my desk chuckling and then reached for the Brooks Brother's bag to put my new socks on and head on home... But the biggest surprise of the day came when I reached into the bag to find that the socks I had purchased were gone...

"Holy fucking fuck," I whispered. "Chris..."

I shouldn't have played so snide with the guy I thought...

It was awfully strange to put my shoes back on with no socks on my feet. I stopped at Brooks Brother's one more time that day before heading home... I used their dressing room to get the new socks on, much to my embarrassment...

The next day I took note of the fact that Chris was wearing a brand new pair of black socks from Brooks Brother's... He laughed softly as I walked past his desk...

The Lifeguard's Red Speedo

I was on volunteer lifeguard duty the summer that this event happened to me. It was totally twisted, if you ask me, horrible trick to have played on a lifeguard. When the community police in the town where I went to college held a seminar on the needs for volunteer lifeguards on the beach I decided to do the right thing and sign up. Being a certified lifeguard how could I not do the right thing and sign up? I was stationed on the beach in the month of August three days a week, including Saturday afternoons from four PM till seven thirty PM. After seven thirty PM the beach is officially closed. I was glad to get the late afternoon schedule, seeing as the beach isn't as crowded during that time as it is in the morning and early afternoons. I was instantly signed up by one of the police officers at the college that day, seeing as I had earned my lifeguard license two summers ago when I had taken a first aid and CPR class. The officer who signed me up thanked me, shook my hand and moved on to the next guy signing up. My afternoons on the beach were pretty boring, although I did meet a few girls, signaling to them to not swim out too far, no swimming near the rocks and no horse play in the water, if you can consider that meeting girls. I never had to rescue someone from drowning, although on the day that I am about to tell you about I thought I was going to rescue some big muscular goof-ball from drowning…

My name is Joe, Joe Andrews to be exact. I'm in my third year of college I'm twenty-three years old. I have silky jet black wavy hair, dark brown eyes and my body is muscular and well toned from all the workouts I put myself through on a daily basis at the college gym. I stand nearly six feet tall and I weigh in at nearly two hundred pounds of sheer bulging muscle. My buddies on campus and in some of my classes call me "Muscled Joe," seeing as every time they see me I'm just coming from a workout at the gym. They tease and razz me a lot those guys, they've nicknamed my biceps "Bowling Balls" and they call my stomach my own personal six pack. My legs have earned themselves the nickname "Tree Trunks."

On the Saturday that I want to tell you about I was on lifeguard duty, sitting atop the two and a half story platform structure set up on the beach. It was five thirty in the afternoon, two more hours to go before I went off duty. Looking around I saw four guys standing on the beach looking around with binoculars. A few times I thought I saw them focusing their binoculars on me, drinking in the sight of me and then handing the binoculars to the next guy. I told myself that I was imagining things. Sitting there in a semi tight fitting (button up at the sides) red Speedo bikini I was really sweating it out and burning in the sun that day. The temperature had hit very high at just above ninety-five degrees and the humidity was one hundred percent. Chugging down mineral water I figured I would take a quick swim and then get right back to my post, seeing as nothing was happening at the moment anyway. The crowd at the beach was starting to disperse as well. At that moment however, while I was contemplating taking a swim I had no idea just how much time I would be spending out in the water. I chugged down some more mineral water and was about to head down from my post when I heard the sounds of yelling from below me.

"Hey, hey you up there, Lifeguard!" a male voice was yelling up to me.

Looking down I saw one of the guys who had been looking around (and at me?) with the binoculars just a few minutes ago.

"Hey Lifeguard, hey big guy, my buddy out there is in trouble!" the lanky blond guy was yelling up at me.

I quickly stood up, grabbed my own binoculars and scanned the area of the ocean he was pointing at, yelling up at me at the same time. As he was yelling up at me about his buddy being in trouble I could have sworn he was drinking in the sight of my crotch as I towered above him on the lifeguard station. I quickly figured I was imagining things. Sure enough, I saw his muscular brown haired buddy thrashing madly in the water, going under and thrashing some more.

"Holy shit," I murmured, put down my binoculars and started down the ladder attached to the lifeguard post. "Relax buddy, I'm on my way!"

"I think he's got the bends," the blond guy yelled and then started running toward the water. "Come on Lifeguard, you got to help him man!"

"I'm right behind you!" I bellowed when my feet hit the hot sand.

I sprinted quickly across the sand and right out into the cold water. Some of the people on the beach were staring at what was happening, but for the most part everyone was pretty much minding their own business. Typical huh? I swam out toward the thrashing guy as fast as possible, right behind the blond guy who had called me down from my post. Fuck, but he was out pretty far I was realizing as I swam and swam toward him. I saw him go under again and it was a few scary seconds till he surfaced again.

"God, he's going to drown," the blond guy yelled back at me.

"He is not going to drown!" I roared back at him.

When I got to where the guy was thrashing in the water I realized just how far out I had swum to get to him. People on the beach seemed very far away to me, as I was to them I was sure.

"Acccchhhhh," the guy was blubbering as he thrashed in the water.

"Hold on man, I'm here, I'm a lifeguard," I said breathlessly as I swam up to him.

I quickly threw my arms around him and bobbing in the water held him slightly aloft. I wanted him to know that everything would be okay now. Then I would see about getting him back to shore, looking around for a stray raft or something to put him on.

"I got you buddy, its okay now," I panted.

The guy looked at me, seemed to get his bearings and smiled with relief.

"Th-thanks man, *shit*, you saved my life," he grunted. "I-I have no idea what happened. Usually I'm a pretty good swimmer. I-I just don't know what happened."

"Hey, it happens to all of us buddy," I said as he clung to me like his life depended upon it.

"Maybe I shouldn't have eaten lunch so soon before going swimming," the muscular guy said to me, holding his arms around my big neck. "All that stuff I heard years ago when I was a kid about getting cramps if you swim after eating must be true huh?"

"Yeah, I would suppose so," I said with a smile as he clung to me tighter still, practically bear hugging me.

Fuck, but I couldn't help but notice that my dick was getting hard in my

Speedo as I held the guy tightly in my strong arms. What was up with that shit anyway? I needed to get him back to the beach that was paramount.

"Is, is he going to be okay?" the blond guy asked, coming up behind me and hooking his arms (for no reason that I could fathom) tightly over my arms as I held his friend aloft and over the water.

"Yeah, he's going to be fine," I said as the blond guy held my arms tighter against me. "Now we just have to get him back to the beach. We're going to have a long swim and…"

Suddenly, as I held the brown haired guy aloft and the blond guy held my arms tight against me I felt hands under the water undoing the buttons on the sides of my Speedo bikini.

"H-hey, wh-what's going on under the water?" I asked, suddenly scared shit-less. "What are you guys up to down there?"

The blond guy held tighter to my arms and the guy I was holding aloft also wrapped his arms around my upper body.

"Don't let me go Lifeguard," he panted desperately.

"B-but, holy shit!" I gasped loudly as I felt my Speedo being pulled down and taken off me under the water.

It was the other two guys who I had seen with the binoculars earlier. They had swum under us while I was supposedly rescuing their buddy and snagged my damned Speedo off me. Surfacing they swam off very fast toward the beach.

"Fuck, *fuck, those bastards just stole my damned swim trunks right off me!*" I snarled angrily.

"Yeah, sure as shit looks that way," the guy in my arms laughed as the blond guy swam off as well. "Thanks a lot for the lift buddy."

With that he gave me a loud, wet, Bugs Bunny type of kiss on the cheek, jumped out of my muscular arms and swam toward the beach with his buddies as well.

"Hey, you bastards!" I roared at them. "Get the fuck back here now with my goddamned swim trunks! Holy shit, I don't believe this!"

I started swimming after them as fast as possible, but stopped dead when I was halfway to the beach. Fuck, I couldn't go up on the sand totally naked, *and* with a raging hard on to boot. I bobbed in the water, watching in rage and helplessness as the four guys swam to the beach. It was the stocky brown haired guy who had my Speedo in hand as he swam. It was the third guy I had seen with the blond guy who had summoned me down from the lifeguard station and the muscular guy I was supposedly rescuing. The fourth guy, from what I could see of him was a handsome tall Spanish guy with an olive complexion and black silky hair.

"Fuck, fuck!" I yelled at the guys. "Get back here you goddamned jokers!"

I watched miserably, as they got up to the sand and then the four of them were standing there looking out at me.

"Come on Lifeguard, come out of the water!" the stocky guy was hooting at me, holding up and waving my Speedo bikini over his head.

"Shit, *shit!*" I rasped, floating myself backward in the water. "Fucking guys, one of you better get out here now with my damned Speedo!"

People on the beach either didn't give a shit or they were simply minding their own business. I suppose they figured that guys always horse around on the beach. I raised a hand clenched into a fist and brought it down hard in the water. The four guys laughed and cackled on the beach. My Speedo in the stocky guy's hand was a sad sight for me to see.

"Come on you guys!" I yelled at them. "You've had your fun. Give me back my damned swim trunks!"

Then, bobbing there in the water I watched as the blond guy and the one I had thought I was rescuing walked back out into the water and swam toward me. On the beach more and more people were starting to leave, seeing as it was getting close to early evening and dinnertime. I watched miserably as any forms of help slowly dispersed. Fuck, not even a goddamned cop around. And even if I could summon a cop what was I going to tell him or her? That some jokesters had tricked me off my lifeguard station and into the water and managed to steal my damned Speedo off me? As the guys got closer to me I floated there in the water, my arms out at my sides.

"Hey there Lifeguard, enjoying the cool water?" the blond guy asked me with a grin. "I think though that it's time you got back to your post."

He and his muscular buddy laughed meanly, slowly circling me like sharks, moving in closer.

"Very funny, *very fucking funny!*" I yelled at them. "Look, you jokers had your goddamned fun, now tell your buddy over there to bring me my goddamned swim trunks so I can get out of the water."

As I spoke the muscular guy who I had rescued swam under the water, out of my sight. The blond guy moved closer to me.

"If he brings me my swim trunks right now I'll just forget this whole thing and…Oooooooo shiiitttt," I began, but my words were suddenly cut off as I felt the muscular guy's mouth and lips close around my hard on under the water.

"H-holy fucking shit and tarnation!" I garbled stupidly, my eyes crossing in my head, goose bumps suddenly breaking out all over me and me feeling breathless in the water. "Th-that fucking guy is s-sucking my damned dick under the water man!"

"Feels good huh Lifeguard?" the blond guy asked me snidely, swimming up to me from behind, hooking his arms around me and reaching for my very erect and cold man tits.

"H-hooooo GAWD, fucking guys, perverts, faggots," I grunted as I was sucked and my man tits were kneaded and twisted.

Then, the guy under the water stopped sucking me and surfaced.

"So that's what this shit was all about huh?" I asked him, as he floated there, facing me with a sly looking grin on his face. "Just wanted to eat some lifeguard meat eh?"

The blond guy let go of me, swam under the water and sucked my hard on into his mouth next.

"Ooooooooo fuckkk, looks like it's your buddy's turn now eh muscle guy?" I asked the brown haired guy.

"Just wanted to show you my appreciation for rescuing me earlier Lifeguard," the guy said, swimming around me and grabbing my man tits just as his blond haired buddy had done.

"F-fuck you man, th-this is a lousy trick you mugs played on me, g-gawd, fucking guy is really sucking my meat stick under the water," I panted breathlessly. "Fucking guy...loves my cock..."

"Yeah, tell me how much you're hating all this Lifeguard," the brown haired guy teased in my ear as he played my tits like they were musical instruments.

But then, like his buddy had done just a few moments prior the blond guy surfaced, coming up in need of air obviously.

"Man, hard as a fucking rock under the water you are Lifeguard," the blond guy said to me, a look of delight on his face. "I guess having your Speedo stolen right off your sexy ass turns you on eh?"

"Fuck you man!" I snarled at him. "Fucking faggots, if your perverted buddy over there on the beach wasn't holding my swim trunks hostage I would make short work of both of you right now."

Then, my words were again cut off as the brown haired guy made his way back under the water and gobbled my manhood into his mouth again.

"Oooooooo fuck, pervert got me by surprise that time," I gasped.

The blond guy held me from behind by my upper arms and swam me further out in the water as his buddy moved me along under the water with my dick in his mouth.

"I-I think I'm goin' to shoot my load man," I gasped suddenly.

The guy under the water suddenly surfaced and he and the blond guy swam off back toward the beach, leaving me way out there in the water, shooting my goddamned load.

"Ohhhhhrrrr gawd, fucking perverts, got me shooting my creamy mess," I grunted throatily. "Ohhhrrrr fuck, fucking A!"

Watching them swim off I reached down, grabbed my spurting dick and gave it a few good yanks and pulls, forcing the last of my gusher out of me.

"Ohhhhhhh yeah, fucked up shit," I mumbled.

Floating on my back, my semi hard dick pointing up from under the water I watched as the two jokers headed to the beach.

"Hey, how long are you assholes planning on keeping me out here for?" I yelled at them. "*Shit!*"

The beach was now pretty much deserted except for the four guys who had tricked me meanly. The sun was starting to set and needless to say I was starting to feel pretty cold. It was about fifteen minutes later when the other two jokers made their way out to me, the two that had actually gotten my swim trunks off me...

"Fuckers, you two come to take your turns tormenting me?" I asked them angrily, looking especially angrily at the brown haired stocky guy, the one who'd had my Speedo in his hand when they swam off. "Where the hell are my swim trunks pervert?"

"Oh, not to worry, they're on the beach with the rest of our stuff Lifeguard," he said to me as his Spanish friend circled me like a hungry shark.

"Yeah?" I asked him. "So when the fuck do I get it back so that I can come up out of the goddamned water?" I'm starting to feel really cold out here man!"

The guy simply snickered and then my eyes crossed in my head as I felt the Spanish guy slurp me into his mouth under the water.

"Ohhhhhhhh, fucking faggots, you guys just love my goddamned meat pole," I gasped. "Bet that's what this was all about huh?"

Smiling, the stocky guy reached and gave my erect and cold nipples a few squeezes as his buddy sucked me off heartily under the water.

"Come on man, give me a break here already," I grunted, thrashing in the water as the Spanish guy ate my manhood like his life depended on it.

"Ohhhhrrrrr gawd, fucking awesome you faggots," I gasped loudly, shooting my load again under the water as the two guys swam off, leaving me there helpless in the water. "Fucking jokers! Ohhhhrrrrr gawd…"

Bobbing there in the water I stroked my manhood, watching helplessly as the two guys swam back to the dark beach where their buddies were waiting…

It was close to seven thirty PM when I started swimming my way to the beach. It was completely deserted at that point and even the four jokers were gone. From where I was I could see that they had left my Speedo lying on the sand. High tide would be coming in soon so I wanted to be off the beach by then.

"Goddamned fuckers," I muttered as I finally put my feet on sand again and walked unsteadily toward where my Speedo was laying on the sand. "What a fucked up trick to play on a lifeguard. Bastards had me out there in the water for close to two hours."

My skin was wet and glistening in the moonlight, totally pruned looking from being in the water for so long. My muscles flexed and spasmed involuntarily in the cool air. That was another nickname I had gained from some of my muscle buddies at the gym, whenever I flexed that way they called me "Flex." My dick was semi hard and my balls had scrunched up in my pink sac, no doubt from being in the cold water for so long. I would be glad to get dressed in the lifeguard's locker room and get back to my dorm room. I bent down, picked up my Speedo and got it back on myself, buttoning it up at the sides. Suddenly, seemingly from out of nowhere the four guys came bounding up to me.

"Good evening Lifeguard," the blond guy snickered.

"H-huh?" I gasped, my feet suddenly off the ground as the four guys hoisted me above their heads by my arms and legs. "H-hey you bastards, put me down, put me the fuck down!"

They lugged me out into the water and literally threw me bodily back in.

"Hooofffffff!" I sputtered, quickly surfacing, ready for anything this time.

But they didn't try to snag my bikini off me a second time. Instead, I saw them hightailing it off the beach…

"Bastards!" I yelled at them, making my way out of the water and to the lifeguard's locker room…

I never saw the four guys again after that…

A Sailor on Leave

It was the fourth of July week-end and the ship that I was stationed on was docked in New York Harbor for all the gala festivities. I had no idea the gala festivities I would soon be enjoying however. I would have two weeks of leave for some fun and enjoyment in my hometown of New York City. Using money I had saved up just for this occasion I would be staying in a room in a hotel in the heart of Times Square. I would look up my two buddies Lester and Joe and invite them up for a few beers and just to spend a little time catching up on things since I had joined the navy two years ago. My name is Steve Grant. I'm a sailor in the U.S. Navy and damned proud of it to say the least. I'm a little over five feet nine inches tall. I have close cut cropped blond hair, blue eyes and I'm pretty muscular and in damned good shape from all the physical training the navy put me through. On the day my ship docked, dressed in my navy whites I made my way in a cab to the luxury hotel where I would be staying where a beautiful room was waiting for me. At the hotel a bellman opened the cab door for me and I stepped out. Before I could grab my heavy duffel bag the bellman took it from the back seat and held it for me as I paid and tipped the driver. When the cab departed I turned to the bellman and smiled at him.

"Welcome to the Grand Diamond hotel Sir," he said to me. "Please follow me to the front desk."

"Thank you," I said with a big smile on my face.

At the desk I gave the gentleman on duty my name and reservation number. He punched a few keys on the computer keyboard in front of him and then asked me for one piece of identification. I showed him my driver's license and he handed me the card key to room number four, zero, five. I turned to the bellman who then led the way to the elevators. He carried my heavy duffel bag like it weighed nothing and then pressed the button with the upward arrow on it.

"Your first time in New York Sir?" he asked me pleasantly.

"No, actually New York is my hometown," I replied with a smile. "I'm here on leave for the Fourth of July holiday and I'm hoping to see a couple of my old friends as well."

"Well good for you Sir," the bellman said to me.

The elevator doors opened and we stepped onto it. The bellman pressed the number four and the doors slid closed. We rode to the fourth floor in silence. A few times I could feel the bellman stealing glances at me. I knew he was queer from the moment he had opened the cab door for me. The way he was gushing over me was obvious that he wanted more than just a tip, the guy wanted to get into my uniform pants. For fun I've let certain buddies of mine in the navy suck my dick and even chow down on my nipples once in a while. One guy I know in the navy loves eating my sweaty raunchy asshole every once in a while. I have to admit that I'm really straight when it comes to sex but when your buddies blindfold you and suck you off it can be any woman you're fantasizing about down there. And who am I to turn down a blowjob once in a while? I'm blessed with a choice A beefy cock so it's no wonder that those guys on my ship are so hypnotized by it at times. My nipples are also of the fleshy robust size so some of my cock sucking sailor buddies see those as a bonus, and as for the guy who likes to eat my asshole, well, "Mangia" I say.

The elevator stopped on the fourth floor and the doors slid open. I followed the bellman down the hall to room four zero five. He placed my duffel bag down on the floor and opened the door for me with his master card key. He stepped aside then so that I could walk in ahead of him. I also got the feeling that he wanted to check out the shape of my ass in my uniform pants.

"Very nice," I said, looking around the room. "Very, very nice…"

"I'm glad you're pleased Sir," the bellman said and put my duffel bag down on the floor at the foot of the king-sized bed.

He seemed to sigh with relief and closed the door to the room.

"Well Sir, if there will be anything else," the bellman said, no doubt expecting the usual tip of a few dollars.

"Well, now that you mention it uh, Mister, uh," I said, walking slowly over to him.

"Bob Sir, my name is Bob," the bellman said and from the look in his eyes I could tell that I had been correct where he was concerned.

"Yes Bob," I said with a wicked looking grin on my face. "There is something else you could do for me…"

Still grinning I stood a few inches from him and took off my pull over white navy jumper, leaving my black neckerchief hanging loose around my big neck. I tossed the jumper on the bed and faced Bob. He looked hungrily at my hairless, big barreled robust chest and my fleshy nipples.

"You know what I could really use about now Bob?" I asked him and squeezed my nipples. "OH man…"

"I uh, I think I do Sir," Bob said eagerly.

I undid the knot in my neckerchief and used it to blindfold myself, just like my buddies on the ship do to me. A second or so later I felt Bob's mouth on my right nipple, his fingers pinching my left nipple.

"Oh yeah Bob, that feels great," I moaned, imagining Bob was a gorgeous woman with red hair and big tits.

He slurped hard at my right nipple, his teeth and tongue and lips really working magic on it while all the while he pinched and tweaked my left nub. He switched over to sucking my left nipple and pinched and squeezed and twisted the right one. He ran his hands down my washboard abs as he sucked my nipples alternately. My cock grew stiff in my uniform pants as I stood there being nipple serviced…

When Bob was done working my big nipples he slid to his knees in front of me. I felt his hands caressing my muscular legs against my uniform pants. He then undid my thirteen buttons at my crotch, pulled my huge cock out of the fly opening in my navy white uniform pants and gobbled the throbber into his mouth. He ran his hands over my thighs as he sucked me and slurped me for all he was worth.

"OHHHHH yeah, that feels really fucking good Bob," I crooned. "I can see a nice tip in store for you when you're done here buddy."

I gyrated my hips as Bob deep throated my manhood, dancing real sexily in front of him as he ate my cock. His lips pressed against the crotch of my pants once he had my entire girth down his throat. He was amazing and talented to be able to swallow all of me like that. When I shot my load Bob gulped it down, swallowing every fucking drop of me. I grunted and swore like a marine, some sailor I am huh? I gave the bellman a large tip and then packed my cock back into my uniform pants. Bob watched as I did up my thirteen crotch buttons. He wished me a pleasant stay in New York and told me to call him if I needed anything else, smacking his lips hungrily as he said it. I promised him that I would do just that and he left the room. With my neckerchief hanging loosely around my neck I flopped down onto the king-sized beautiful bed and stretched out. I squeezed my jutted up nipples and laughed.

"Fuckin' queer bastard," I whispered, thinking of Bob. "I'll have you up here every fucking day to chow down on my fuck meat…"

That night I called my friend Lester on the phone. He picked up on the third ring.

"Hello?" Lester said.

"Hey Lester you bastard, guess who?" I asked him.

"Steve baby!" Lester shouted into the phone. "When the fuck did you get into town?"

"This morning," I replied. "I'm staying at the Grand Diamond. Why don't you and Joe come up tomorrow? We can all spend the day together."

"Sounds good buddy," Lester said. "We have a surprise for you by the way."

"Oh yeah, what is it?" I asked him eagerly.

"Keep your navy issued underpants on buddy, you'll find out tomorrow," Lester responded sternly. "Believe me buddy, you'll love it."

"Okay, I'll take your word on that, and I will keep my navy issued underpants on…"

We both laughed and then Lester asked me how the navy was treating me.

"Same as usual," I replied. "I heave my guts up over the side of the ship every fucking night of the week."

"With your stomach I don't know why the fuck you decided to join the goddamned navy," Lester laughed.

"Because I don't look good in army green, I hate heights and the marines are all psychos, SIR!" I yelled heartily into the phone.

Lester and I laughed again…

"Listen Sailor boy, we'll see you tomorrow at say ten in the morning, that work for you?" Lester asked me.

"Sure thing Bro," I said and we both paused for a second or two.

"It's good to hear from you buddy," Lester said.

"Same here man," I said and we hung up.

I leaned back on the bed, unlaced my spit polished black patent leather shoes and yanked them off my size ten feet. I placed the shoes on the floor, crossed my feet in front of me and closed my eyes. As I laid there I thought about how lucky I was to have two such good friends as Lester and Joe. I would never forget how they helped me through the worst time in my life…when my parents and my sister (my only sibling) had been killed in a senseless car crash a few years ago. Lester and Joe were my family whenever I came home to visit New York City. My eyes filled with tears and I drifted into a semi sleep…

The next morning…

I woke up at eight AM on the dot, showered, shaved and took care of other usual bathroom needs. I had Bob the bellman bring me a large coffee, a few bagels and juice for breakfast. Before I ate I had Bob suck me off. After he left the room I sat down and ate two bagels and drank half the coffee. At five after ten I was watching television when I heard a knock at my hotel room door. I clicked off the television and walked over to the door.

"Who is it?" I called out.

"Who the fuck do you think it is?" a familiar voice called out in response from the other side of the door.

I unlocked the door and threw it open. Standing there with huge smiles on their faces were Lester and Joe.

"Hey you two!" I cried out happily.

"Stevey boy!" Lester whooped and grabbed me in a bear hug.

He hoisted me off the floor and carried me into the room as Joe came in carrying a backpack. Joe closed the door as Lester trotted around the room with me still hoisted in his grasp.

"Fucking strong fucker you've become," I said, looking down at Lester.

Chuckling, he put me down on the floor and the two men looked me over in all my uniformed glory.

"Damn you look great Steve," Joe said as he shook hands with me and then hugged me. "You really do justice to that uniform…"

"Thanks Joe," I said with a smile. "That's a real nice compliment…"

"You doin' okay buddy?" Lester asked me and squeezed the back of my neck. "They treating you alright in the damned navy?"

"I'm fine Lester," I said slowly. "Really…"

Both of us choking back tears we grabbed each other and hugged tight. Lester placed his hand on the back of my peach fuzzed head and held me tight.

"It's good to see you Steve," Lester choked.

A while later we were all sitting out on the terrace sipping cups of coffee as we talked over things, catching up on stuff, and filling each other in on what was new in our lives.

"So, I want to know about this surprise you mentioned on the phone last night," I said to Lester. "What the fuck is it already?"

"Should we tell him?" Lester asked Joe.

"I don't see why not," Joe said and grinned at Lester.

"We went into business together," Lester said to me.

For a moment we were all silent and then I smiled.

"Congratulations guys!" I said. "What kind of business is it?"

"Well, it's a …" Joe began.

"No, no…" Lester said, cutting off Joe's words. "It's better if we show you. Lets go back inside."

We all stood up and stepped back into my hotel room. Joe picked up the backpack and placed it on the writing table.

"You ready Steve?" Joe asked me.

"Sure," I said anxiously.

"Wait, wait!" Lester said, grabbing my arm. "Let's blindfold him first. You got something we could blindfold you with Steve?"

"Sure do," I said and undid my neckerchief.

I handed Lester the black neckerchief and he tied it over my eyes. I then heard Joe open his backpack and objects were being placed on the table we were standing in front of.

"What is this all about?" I asked with a smile. "What the hell kind of business did you two open up?"

A few moments later Lester took the blindfold off me. I looked down at the table and saw an assortment of items. I saw a pair of nipple clamps with very sharp looking teeth on them, ball bearings of various sizes with long strings attached to them, various paddles made of leather, and handcuffs. I looked over the items on the table and then looked at the two men standing at my sides. I smiled knowingly.

"Oh shit…" I said. "OH fucking shit…you two have opened one of those S&M stores just like the Pink Pussycat and The Pleasure Chest."

"Bingo Steve!" Lester said happily and slapped my ass hard. "And business is booming Stevey boy. We are getting rich fast!"

I grinned and picked up one of the leather paddles.

"Shit, I bet this hurts when it connects with a butt good and hard huh?" I asked them.

"Why don't you find out?" Lester said, grinning fiendishly at me.

"I-uh, I don't know man…" I said. "Probably I would be able to take it but I really don't know…"

"I have an idea," Joe said.

"What's that?" I asked him.

"Let's all draw cards," Joe said as a suggestion. "The guy with the smallest value card has to let the other two work him over with all this shit for as long as they want to. He has to let them do whatever they want to him and he has to obey all their commands."

"I don't know Joe…" I said.

"I'll do it," Lester said as Joe took a deck of playing cards out of the backpack. "Come on Steve, it might be fun. Maybe you and I will get to stomp Joe all day."

"Yeah…maybe…" I said and suddenly I was smiling very fiendishly.

We watched Joe shuffle the cards and then place them down on the table with the erotic items. Lester went first, picking a card from the bottom of the deck. I went next and took the card at the top of the deck. Joe pulled a card from the middle of the deck. None of us had looked at our cards yet.

"Okay, once we look at and show our cards there's no turning back," Joe said sternly. "Deal?"

"Deal," Lester said.

"Deal," I said a little nervously.

We all looked at our cards. My heart sunk faster than the Titanic did. Lester held up a king of diamonds. Joe held up an ace of clubs. I gulped hard.

"What do you have buddy?" Lester asked me, knowing full well I was the big loser in this game.

I held up a ten of clubs. The two men gave each other a high five, cackled like two teenagers, and took turns slapping my bubble butt...

"You guys knew I would lose..." I said, trying to put up a brave front.

"It's a chance we took Stevey boy," Lester said and clapped me on the back. "Now, strip that pretty uniform of yours off down to your shoes and socks..."

"WHAT???" I asked him.

"Remember," Joe said, looking at me with authority showing in his face. "You have to do whatever we tell you to..."

I grimaced, not feeling so smug anymore, and took off my pullover jumper. I pulled my uniform pants off over my shoes and socks and then pulled off my underpants, also over my shoes and socks. I placed my clothes neatly on a chair and looked at my two buddies. They seemed to be drooling as they looked at my muscular and hairless body.

"Man oh fucking man Stevey boy, the navy has worked wonders with you," Lester said and grabbed a handful of my bubble butt, squeezing it hard. "Just look at the fucking build on you…"

Joe stepped to the other side of me and tweaked and twisted one of my meaty nipples.

"Stand at attention Sailor boy," Joe said to me with total authority in his voice. "Hands behind your back…"

I did as I was told, following orders and abiding by the instructions of the game. My heart was pounding like mad in my chest and my dick started getting hard as my two buddies ran their hands over me. They squeezed my butt cheeks and tweaked and squeezed the bejesus out of my nipples. There was something real intense about all this, being enslaved by two guys that were your best buds in the entire world.

"When did you two become faggots?" I asked them through clenched teeth as they handled me.

"Come on Stevey boy you're goin' to tell us that you've never fooled around with other guys?" Lester asked me and picked up the handcuffs. "Bein' in the navy and all…must get pretty lonely out there on a ship, all those months, all you guys with no women around…"

I didn't reply and he snapped the handcuffs onto my wrists, locking my hands behind me. Lester and Joe proceeded to touch and handle me in every possible sexy place, squeezing and slapping my butt cheeks hard, tugging on my erect dick and hanging balls, tweaking my nipples painfully and twisting them, and slapping my hard, flat washboard stomach region. The sounds of slapping reverberated in the hotel room.

"UUUUHHHHRRRR…" I moaned.

"Man oh man, he has some fuckin' muscle boy body," Lester said to Joe.

They each slurped one of my nipples into their mouths and began sucking them hard. I didn't ask to be blindfolded this time around…my situation was bad/good enough as it was. I watched as Lester and Joe feasted heartily on my big nipples, chewing on them, bighting on them, and licking them, GAWD, did they lick my nipples. As they worked my nipples my dick throbbed long and beefy and hard. In a very short while those nipples of mine were erect, hard and pointy, just the way Lester and Joe wanted them. They stopped working my nubs and Joe picked up the tit clamps. He opened them all the way and I have to say that the teeth on those things looked pretty sharp. They were hungry those teeth, they were hungry for a sailor boy's nipples.

"Hold still now and stay standing at attention Sailor boy," Joe said to me as he brought the tit clamps toward my nipples.

I cringed in fear and anticipation and grimaced in pain even before the clamps were clipped to my nipples. Then, they were on my nipples and Joe was screwing them shut tighter and tighter.

"AAHHHRRRRR fuck, this shit hurts you guys!" I roared.

"We haven't even gotten started yet," Lester said as Joe went on tightening the screws on the tit clamps.

"FUCKERS!" I yelled. "Why did I let myself get into this???"

"Too late to back out now," Joe said meanly and finished screwing the tit clamps onto my poor nipples. "No backing out, remember?"

"Yeah, I fucking remember," I seethed angrily. "My best friends…"

Lester picked up a round leather paddle, rubbed it against my butt cheeks, and whacked me hard with it.

"YOWWWWCHH!" I screamed and almost lost my at attention stance.

Lester walked over to the couch, sat down and told me to come over to him. Slowly, I walked over to him, knowing all too well what the fuck I was in for. Seconds later Lester had me over his knees, my butt right over his lap and a ready target for his round leather paddle.

"Okay you hot sailor boy, how many swats should we start you off with?" Lester asked me jokingly and whacked my ass hard with the leather paddle.

"YOWWWWCHHH!" I screamed again. "That's enough already!"

"Now, now, don't be cocky Sailor boy," Lester said and whacked my ass again.

"YOWWWWCCHHH!" I cried out.

"I have an idea," Lester said happily. "We'll use the cards! Joe, would you be so kind as to pick out a number card from the deck?"

Joe smiled a wicked smile and picked the top card off the deck. He held it up and we saw that it was a six of clubs.

"Six hard ones coming up," Lester said and brought the damned paddle down on my butt...hard. "Or perhaps I should say six hard ones going down..."

"YOWWWCCHHH!" I screamed over and over as Lester paddled my butt six times in a row...mercilessly it seemed.

Between the pain from the clamps on my nipples and the paddling I was getting I was slowly regretting all this. I had come to New York for a vacation and instead I was being worked over by my two best buddies in the whole world. At the same time there was something intoxicating about it all. I was a definite mixture of emotions at that moment. A few moments later I found myself lying across Joe's knees. He had the leather paddle in hand and watched intently as Lester picked a card from the deck. He held up a nine of diamonds.

"Nine hard and painful ones coming up Sailor boy," Joe said and began beating my butt with the paddle. Again I screamed in pain as the paddle began to sting as it connected with my tender butt cheeks. I pleaded with Joe to take it a little easier, a little slower maybe, but instead my pleas fueled his drive and caused him to paddle me harder and harder. The nine blows seemed to go on and on forever but finally it was done.

"Man, your butt cheeks sure are red and wounded looking Stevey boy," Joe said and squeezed my cheeks hard.

"OUCCHHH!" I bellowed.

Moments later I was lying on my king-sized bed on my stomach, my hands still cuffed behind me, and my feet spread far apart and bound at the ankles to the legs of the bed. My dick and balls were pulled under me, fully exposed and real sexy looking. The clamps on my nipples were torturing me even more now because I was lying against them. I squirmed miserably on the bed as my two buddies stood on either side of me, both of them holding a riding crop in their hands.

"Okay Joe, these things will hurt even more than the paddle did so we want to get it over as quickly as possible," Lester said, sounding like he actually meant it. "So, lets pick our numbers and whack him quickly but effectively.

Lester brought his riding crop down on my ass, hard, as a sampling blow.

"AAAYYRRR!" I screamed and my muscular body jerked upward on the bed.

The riding crop stung ten times more than the leather paddles did. GAWD, what had I let myself in for??? Joe placed the ever present deck of cards between my spread legs on the bed ad picked up the top one. It was a four of diamonds. Joe tossed the card down and raised his riding crop high over my ass cheeks.

"Please...take it easy..." I pleaded, my eyes filling with tears.

Joe whacked my ass cheeks four times really hard and brutally with the riding crop. With each blow I screamed loud in pain and my body jerked up and down on the bed. My nipples rubbed painfully against the bed as did my rock hard cock. I realized that all through the pain I was feeling my cock remained stalwart and erect. I also realized that I was being made to jack myself off as my two buddies beat my ass with the riding crops. When Joe was done Lester wasted no time in picking a card from the deck. My tears flowed when he held up a ten of diamonds.

"OHHHHRRR FUCK..." I whimpered loudly and buried my face against the bed.

Lester whacked my butt hard and the pain shot through me like a train going at one hundred miles an hour. When he had reached only the fifth swat I was crying loudly against the bed sheets, screaming in pain, and shaking violently. He quickly gave me the last five whacks, grabbed my hard dick, stroked it a few times, and I shot a hefty load onto the bed.

"OOOHHHHHHH fuck, oooooooo shit man..." I cried, my head raised up off the bed and looking back as Lester stroked my crank harder and harder. "OHHHHH GAWD, fuckin' making me shoot my damned load after torturing me and all...WHAT A FEELING..."

When I was done cumming Lester let go of my dick and he and Joe rubbed some soothing aloe lotion onto my ass cheeks, massaging it in…

"AHHH, that feels nice," I said, managing a small smile.

A few minutes later I was off the bed and standing in the center of the room again. I was at rigid attention, my hands still cuffed behind me and the clamps still on my nipples. Lester and Joe were standing at my sides, rubbing their hands over and over my rock hard chest. They prodded my bellybutton with their fingertips and squeezed my pecs and nipples hard.

"Okay Sailor boy, time for the next round…" Joe said. "And don't think we're done whacking you…"

I gulped and watched as the two men each picked up a ball bearing with a string attached to them.

"Oh shit guys, what the fucking fuck am I in for now???" I croaked miserably.

"Just stand at attention and don't fucking move," Joe said into my face.

Together the two men knelt in front of me and they each began tying the strings attached to the ball bearings around my balls. They were really rough about it too as they manhandled my poor testicles.

"AARRRRRHHH…" I seethed, trying to remain standing at attention.

When they were done tying the ball bearings to my balls both men were each holding the heavy metal balls in their fingers.

"Okay Sailor boy, when we let go of these you're going to feel a pain shoot through you like none you've ever known before," Joe said threateningly. "When you feel that pain you can stand down at ease, if you're standing at all that is…"

"Guys no, no…" I cried pitifully.

They let go of the ball bearings and the devices pulled painfully and agonizingly on my poor balls.

"AAARRRHHHH!" I roared and doubled over in pain. "OHHHHHH SHIT you guys! My poor fucking nuts!"

As I stood there doubled over the two men, my two best buddies in the whole world, (HA!) each picked up their riding crops.

"Start walking around the table Sailor boy," Lester instructed me. "Each time you make it around full circle you'll receive two good hard swats on some part of that gorgeous body of yours."

"OH JEEZ, lucky me, h-how many times do I have to walk around the table???" I asked as I headed over to the table still doubled over.

It felt like I was dragging my balls along with me as the ball bearings pulled down on them unforgivingly. I was crying like a baby now and snot was dripping out of my nose and onto my trembling lips. I was sweating profusely at that point and I smelled ripe from fear.

"We'll shoot for twenty times around the table but if after ten it looks like you're in unendurable pain we'll let you stop," Lester said. "Now get moving…"

I began walking around the table slowly, still doubled over in pain. As I made my way around the table the two men reached out with their riding crops and whacked me with them…hard. They got me on my muscular arms, my ass cheeks, (again) my thighs, my legs and my broad shoulders. By the time I was up to the tenth walk around the table I was dripping with sweat from head to toe, my hair was matted to my head, I had red marks all over me from the riding crops and I was in a sort of daze. I stopped walking, trying to catch my breath…

"Move it!" Joe yelled at me and raised his riding crop.

"JOE, stop!" Lester said demandingly and rushed over to me.

He took me by my upper arms and walked me over to the couch. The two men quickly took the clamps off my nipples and the ball bearings off my balls. One of them put a glass of cold water to my lips and I sipped it, thanking them in between sips. A while later the handcuffs were off me and I was still sitting between my two buddies on the couch as they were gently rubbing my arms, my shoulders, my chest and my nipples.

"Feelin' okay?" Lester asked me.

"Yeah, I'm alright, I guess," I said, looking down at my semi hard dick. "I hope it still works…"

"You're a tough sailor boy Steve," Lester said. "You sure as hell can take it."

"Yeah, I sure as shit can," I replied and smiled. "Thanks for the demonstration guys…I suppose…"

"After you're honorably discharged from the navy and if you need a job you can come and work with us," Joe suggested.

"Oh yeah?" I asked him. "Doing what?"

"We'll use you to demonstrate the merchandise for the customers…" Joe said and we all laughed hysterically.

I spent the rest of the Fourth of July holiday relaxing with my two buddies and we all had a great time in Manhattan.

When I got back to my ship I still had my special buddies blindfold me and suck me off. The only difference now is that while I'm being sucked off in blindfolded darkness I think about my buddies Lester and Joe and what they did to me while I was enjoying my Fourth of July holiday in New York City…

Thanks guys, you two are the fucking best.

Licking Arthur's Feet at the Office

Note from the author: My classic story, "Licking Arthur's Feet" appeared in my first book, "The Executive Guide to Foot Fetishism and Office Discipline." That story introduced handsome office executive, Arthur and his foot and sock worshipping buddy Brad. The story showed how two men could come to realize a mutual foot fetish. It also showed the ever-present mystery that seems to surround some men's lust and love for another man's feet... This quick sequel follows the antics of the two executives during the workday in Arthur's private office...

It was twelve thirty PM and most of the staff at the bank where I work was out to lunch, or headed to lunch as I headed toward Arthur's office on that Monday. I had some papers and documents that I needed him to sign before I sent them out to the vice president of our bank branch. When I got to Arthur's office I knocked twice on the door and then slowly opened it. I stuck my head in and saw Arthur sitting behind his desk talking on the phone. To my joy he had his feet propped up on his desk. My breath caught in my throat as he smiled at me. He waved me in and continued his conversation on the phone. I closed Arthur's office door, locked it and slowly walked over to his desk, my eyes riveted to his feet propped up on his desk. Arthur was wearing black lace-up wingtip shoes and black ribbed nylon dress socks with his charcoal colored suit that day. I placed the papers and documents to be signed on the desk next to Arthur's feet and sat down in the chair facing him.

"Yeah, don't worry Marty," Arthur said to the person on the other end of the phone. "The new system is working fine so far. I went over it myself with my good buddy Brad here; he's a real boy wonder I have to say.

As Arthur spoke I reached forward and ran my hands over his highly polished wingtip shoes, pressing my thumbs against his ankles, feeling the hardness of them, loving the feel of his black nylon socks against his skin.

"Arthur…" I whispered and leaned my face close to his feet.

I kissed Arthur's shoes a few times, licked the toes sections of them and inhaled their heady leathery aroma.

"Yeah, uh, he's here now as a matter of fact," Arthur said to Marty on the phone. "And from the look of things we're going to have a working lunch hour…"

Arthur smiled from ear to ear as I began unlacing his shoes. I did it reverently, slowly unlacing his wingtips. When the laces were undone I sucked them a bit. Then, slowly and methodically I pulled Arthur's wingtips off his feet and sniffed the inside of each shoe heavily. The insides of Arthur's shoes smelled musty and pungent at the same time. He continued speaking to Marty as he watched me lick the insides of his shoes a few times. Then, I placed Arthur's shoes on the floor and wrapped my hands around one of his socked feet, massaging it, squeezing it.

"Uh Marty, I better go," Arthur said as I began licking the tips of his socked toes, nipping at them.

"Yeah, Brad is starting to eat lunch already, Okay, I'll talk to you soon…"

He hung up the phone and leaned back in his chair, a look of sheer contentment on his handsome face. He crossed his hands over his chest and watched intently as I sucked on his socked toes one at a time, holding his foot tightly in my hand. The sounds of slurping filled the air around me, as did the leathery and silky scent of Arthur's black dress socks.

"Jeez Brad, you just can't wait to get at those smelly feet of mine," Arthur said with a shit eating grin on his face. "Go ahead Brad, lick and suck those socks of mine."

"God almighty Arthur," I whispered, looking up at him with his foot in my hands, my thumbs caressing the bottoms of them. "I wish I could understand it somehow…I just love your feet…"

I pressed my face against the bottom of his socked foot and sniffed heavily and heartily, taking in the odor of Arthur's foot sweat and his sock. My cock grew hard in my suit pants. I licked the bottom of Arthur's foot, pressing my tongue against it for all I was worth. I drooled over the top of his foot and then sucked my saliva off it. I yanked the tips of his socks slightly away from his toes and sucked the juicy sweat from the material of them. YUM. Then, I licked around Arthur's ankle and again sucked his toes, this time having a mouthful of sock as well. I moved to his other foot and went to work on that one next, sniffing it like crazy, kissing the sides of it over and over, and licking the bottom of it. Arthur hiked up his suit pants some more, revealing more of his ribbed black nylon socks.

"Go for it Brad," Arthur said, still grinning from ear to ear. "Lick my socks buddy…"

I grabbed Arthur by his ankles and ran my tongue up and down his long ribbed socks, kissing them along the way. When I reached the tops of his socks I held one of his legs around the calf and the bottom of his glorious foot.

"Knee length socks eh? OTC..." I asked him teasingly. "Fucking hot executive feet you have Arthur..."

I ran my hands lovingly over Arthur's socks, warming his feet as I did so, adoring the feel of the sweaty nylon material against his legs.

Moments later Arthur was kneeling in his chair, facing backward, his heels available to me. I knelt on the floor at his feet and ran my tongue over Arthur's heels, drooling over them, and licking up the saliva as it trailed down the bottoms of his glorious feet.

"OHHHH man, that feels so good," Arthur moaned contentedly. "Lick my heels Brad, bight on them; suck the fuck out of them..."

Arthur held onto the back of his chair as I did as he asked. His pants were still hiked up to his knees so I was able to hold onto his socked calves as I worked on his heels and the bottoms of his feet. I even squeezed my nipples under my dress shirt as I serviced Arthur's feet...

But alas, all good things must come to an end, and so did lunch hour. When time was up I put Arthur's wingtips back onto his feet and tied the laces for him. I gave his shoed feet a few final kisses and licks and then he signed the papers I had brought into his office, his feet now under his desk.

"Thanks Arthur," I said softly.

"For what?" he asked me. "For signing the papers or for letting you lick and kiss my damned smelly socks?"

"For both," I replied.

As I was walking toward the door of Arthur's office he called my name. I turned around and looked at him. His feet were back up on his desk.

"My wife is going to be out of town tonight Brad," Arthur said to me, grinning slyly and rubbing his ankles together. "Maybe before you head home you may want to stop over. My socks will no doubt need another working on, not to mention my bare feet…"

I nodded "yes", looking hungrily at Arthur's feet…

About the Author

Christopher Trevor

Christopher Trevor was born in July 1963 and grew up in New York City. As soon as he was old enough to know how he began writing fiction and has been writing gay erotic/ fetish stories for the past ten to twelve years at this point. He became an avid reader as well from the time he knew how and reads everything from fiction, to non-fiction to biographies of interesting and unusual people, people who have made a difference or who have paved the way for others. Christopher attributes his writing artistic inspiration to artists such as Etienne, Tom of Finland, Tagame, The Hun, and most notably

Joe T, who Christopher has had the pleasure of speaking with and even meeting over the last few years. Christopher states, "Joe T encouraged me to write about my fetish because I was embarrassed about it at the time. Joe T said that when we

are embarrassed about something that makes it even more enticing somehow." Christopher totally agreed and never stopped writing in this genre. Erotic writers who inspired Christopher Trevor were: Tom Shaw (author of "That Day at the Quarry), C.S. White (author of Big Sur), Larry Townsend (author of countless erotic novels), and Mason Powell (author of the classic story "The Brig.")

Christopher discovered that not only did he enjoy writing erotic tales but that after his first bondage experience he had a genuine flair for it. Writing to erotic oriented magazines about his first bondage experience truly opened the floodgates for Christopher where this style of writing is concerned. Christopher thanks the handsome and muscular "Greg" for that experience way back in time. Christopher took "Creative Writing" courses every semester during his high school years and while other friends of his stopped writing what they loved to write about as time went on Christopher never let a day go by when he didn't write something... "I feel that if I don't write every day I will die," Christopher has said many times over.

Foot fetish stories and all things related; spanking fetish, erotic shaving, muscle bondage, tickle torture, and hardcore stories are just a few of the areas of gay eroticism that Christopher enjoys writing about and inspiring in others as well. As one internet buddy said to Christopher where the black socks fetish is concerned, "Until I started talking with you I never gave a thought to my socks when I got dressed for work in the morning. Now when I pull my dress socks on every morning I get a chill up my spine."

Christopher is proud of the erotic effect he has on people...

Christopher Trevor is also the author of:

The Executive Guide to Foot Fetishism and Office Discipline
1-887895-36-1

Executive Ties That Bind
1-887895-37-X

Don't! Stop! That Tickles!
1-887895-31-0

The Taming of Dominick
1-887895-45-0

Timmy and The Hong Kong Tailor
1-887895-30-2

Love, Torture and Redemption
1-887895-32-9

Timmys Ticklish Trials
978-1-887895-74-3

The Gym Instructor
978-1-887895-44-6

Milked
978-1-887895-66-8

Erotic Street Blues
978-1-887895-97-2

The Abusive Wager
978-1-887895-04-0

Terry's Appointment and Other Tickling Stories
978-1-934625-08-8

The Military File
978-1-934625-21-7

Quirks
978-1-934625-24-8

Timmy and the Evil Dr. Vonvellicator
978-1-934625-42-2

Blackmail
978-1-934625-47-7

Tickled Kink
978-1-934625-49-1

Look for them where you bought this book or TheNazcaPlainsCorp.com

www.ingramcontent.com/pod-product-compliance
Lightning Source LLC
Chambersburg PA
CBHW051129260626
47170CB00005B/1737